Second Chances

When Life Sends You Lemons

by

Lois Gerber, RN, BSN, MPH

Riggs & Sons Publications
Daytona Beach, Florida

Other books by Lois Gerber

Nadia: Poland
Nadia: Detroit
Runaway Girl: A Nurse's Story
The Human Side of Nursing
Nurses and Their Patients: Acts of Courage and Conviction
Nurses and Their Patients: Compassion and Commitment
New Beginnings

Author Website

http://nursesbookshelf.com

Table of Contents

Shooting Under Par

Summer in northern Michigan is the best time of the year. On a warm August afternoon in Traverse City, Dad's standing on the first tee. My older brother, Mike, sits beside me in the golf cart waiting to hit the ball next. Then it's my turn. I take a deep breath and run my fingers through my blond hair. This will be my last golf game of the season with my family.

Tomorrow I'll be living in Detroit, in an apartment off Cass Avenue close to Wayne State University where I've transferred my local community college credits. I want to earn an easy degree, so I picked communications as my major. Last month on my twenty-first birthday, realizing I've been in a rut after breaking up with my high-school girlfriend, I vowed to do something different, like moving to one of the country's biggest cultural "melting pots" in the inner city to take advantage of the student loan I'd received.

"I'm going to miss you guys and, of course, golf," I say.

Mike nudges me on the shoulder. "You'll be home for Thanksgiving, if not sooner, Dan. Your classes won't last forever. Plus we'll try to visit. We know the way."

I shrug. "I'm just not sure it's the right decision. I'll have a butt load of debt, and I hear the golf courses aren't as good down there. Let's hope I like it."

"Aw, come on," Dad chimes in with his two cents. "You'll be back on some course sharpening up for the U.S. Open in no time and have more college credits under your belt."

Mike slips on his golf glove. "In a few years you'll be the golf pro you've talked about since you were a kid and enough cash to pay off your student loan."

I run my hand over my forehead. "Yeah," I mutter. "Nice thought, but you're the lucky one who got the full ride to the University of Michigan."

Two years ago, Mike graduated with honors from U of M's nursing program. After working a year on a medical floor, he recently took a job in a local hospital emergency room. I envy his dedication to school and high grades and his work. Me? I'm smart enough but always put fun first. Thus, no scholarships, at least not this year.

He sighs. "To be honest, I feel guilty having taken all that money when you didn't get any."

"Not to worry. The school made a good investment in you." I laugh to lighten the mood.

Dad hits the ball. A nice drive. "You're up, Mike," he hollers.

I take a deep breath as my brother walks to the tee and swings his driver a few times to warm up. I put on my glove and step up to the tee box.

Mike and I both hit nice drives. We play a relaxed game, joke a lot, and drink a few beers. I end the round three strokes over par.

***

It's 1:30 AM the week before Halloween. I'm sitting alone at the bar in the Raven's Lounge in Detroit's Midtown. I come to hear some blues and meet Alicia, a gal who sits behind me in my English literature class. She's about my age and styles her dark hair in a ponytail. Tonight she's wearing a short jean skirt frayed at the hemline and a V-neck white sweater. I buy her three drinks and talk to her for over two hours. She compliments me on my cute smile and the sexy twinkle in my eyes.

To me that deserves a good lay, but she doesn't see it that way. When she asks me to walk her the several blocks to her car, I think maybe she'll change her mind. So I try to kiss her and maybe in the process accidentally touch her boobs, I don't know. Anyway, she gets really pissed off and pushes me so hard I almost fall.

"Screw you," I say and amble back toward the bar for another beer. I put Alicia out of my mind and let my thoughts wander to golf, my passion. I see myself hitting the perfect shot, 300 yards down the center of the fairway. I'm going to turn pro someday, but I need to get my handicap down at least three strokes.

The next thing I know, two guys jump me from behind. One jams a gun into my ribs. "Don't try anything, asshole. Just give me your wallet." His voice is raspy.

No goddamn way anyone is going to rob me. I turn quickly and hit hard on his right temple, then another jab to the left. He drops to the ground. His friend picks up his handgun and runs.

Minutes later, Alicia and a cop are headed my way. The cute skirt and sweater she wore are torn and her hair is messed. She wags her finger at me, then stares at the policeman. "He got mad when I wouldn't go to bed with him. He pushed me into the backseat of my SUV, smacked me around, then tried to rape me." She points to the man I just hit who is now lying on the ground. "That's a neighbor down my street. I don't know his name. I watched the whole thing. Dan here tried to rob him. When the man resisted, Dan punched him hard."

I gasp.

The sound of shrieking sirens fills the air. An ambulance and fire engine arrive simultaneously. The EMT kneels to tend to the injured man, who's dressed in faded jeans and a black sweatshirt. He looks older than me, probably in his thirties. We both have athletic builds although he looks about twenty pounds heavier.

My heart pounds. Perspiration drips from my forehead. The man isn't moving. God, did I kill him?

"What's your side of the story, mister?" the policeman asks.

"It's all a lie. I did try to kiss the girl but never smacked her around. And then two men jumped me." I point to the guy on the ground. "He pushed a gun in my ribs, demanded my wallet. I hit him with my fist and he fell. There's no blood."

The EMT looks up. "He's gone."

"I didn't mean to hurt him bad, let alone kill him. I'm sorry. It was self-defense."

"Not according to our witness. You're under arrest until we get this sorted out, the cop says."

The officer handcuffs me and leads me to the police car, where another cop sits behind the wheel. He shoves me in the back seat and locks me up behind wire mesh that separates the front and back of the sedan. I cower in the corner of the smooth vinyl seat and brace myself when the car makes sharp turns. I sob harder than I did when I was ten and our cocker spaniel died.

***

Finally, the car stops with a jolt. The officer opens the rear door to let me out. I stumble in front of him as he leads me into a small room with several folding chairs and a glassed-in cubicle with a grapefruit sized opening. "Sit here. Carla will take care of you," he says. "In case you want to know, you're in the Wayne County Jail."

The heavy-set Hispanic woman behind the glass wears a black and gray uniform. My hands shake. I swallow down bile, praying I don't puke. Carla speaks softly and looks at me kindly as she collects my identifying information. I relax even as she takes my wallet, cell phone, and car keys. "Your things will be in this bag. You'll get them back when you're released," she says.

Next, I'm taken to a mini-clinic where, three minutes later, a nurse takes my blood pressure and pulse and listens to my heart. "You're good to go," she says.

Another officer fingerprints and photographs me. I had read about strip searches, but when his finger goes up my ass, my mind goes blank, my thoughts so jumbled that nothing makes sense. I try to talk, but the words don't come out. Somehow, I put on the orange jump suit and soft slippers the officer gives me. "I'm putting your street clothes in the bag with your other things," he says.

When he takes me to the upper bunk in my cell, I plop down on the thin mattress, curl up in a ball facing the wall, and weep. I'm shivering even though it's not cold.

The hours that follow are a nightmare. I am allowed to use the jail corded phone to call home and ask my family for help. They are shocked but promise to find a good attorney. Mike says the family is upset, that the local news is covering the story non-stop and that he will be down the following day.

I spend most of the time lying on the cell's upper bunk. The musty smell often makes me cough. God help me, please! I think of Mom, Dad, my friends and golf buddies. I don't want to be here. I'm too young, haven't even started to live. I want to go home.

Mike visits. I get to talk to him for twenty minutes through a glass wall via a phone. He and Dad have hired a criminal lawyer, Frank Holloway. We meet several times over the next several weeks and talk. I tell him all that happened. He takes notes on his iPad. He believes my side of the story and works to get witnesses to support my claim.

Instead of spending Thanksgiving with my family, I sit in jail waiting for a trial scheduled for early January. The bastards deny me bail, saying I'm a danger to society. How is that possible?

I have little appetite for the greasy institution-like food served with plastic utensils and paper plates, I've lost weight. I'm exhausted during the day as I wake up nights in a cold sweat, my heart pounding from the ghoulish memories of the arrest. Sometimes, I wake up screaming. When several gang members from the Aryan Brotherhood threaten me, I'm put in solitary confinement for my own protection.

This can't be happening. In my wildest imagination, I never thought I'd end up like this, I ache all over. A guard, a gangly middle-aged man, brings me my meals on a tray he slides through a small opening in the door that shuts from the outside. The cell, probably ten by twelve has no windows. A stainless-steel toilet and small sink combo fill a corner.

I lie on my cot and mull over the survival strategies I learned in Boy Scouts. The one I liked best was *to think of something to visualize, something important to you, something to take you away from your situation.* For me that has to be golf at the new thirty-six-hole course in Traverse City, an hour's drive north of Saginaw....

It's a warm day in May. I drive to the course with the windows open in my crimson red Pontiac. Trees covered with white cherry blossoms line the highway. The air is fragrant; the sun is shining. I smile. I park and grab my white leather Nikes from the back seat and sit on the bumper to put on my metal spikes. Shoes changed, I pull my golf bag out of the trunk and sling it over my shoulder, then set the bag down in the courses' drop area while I walk to the Pro Shop to pay and find out my tee time. There is a group ahead of me, so I glance at the new clubs and gloves for sale. I think about buying the expensive *Top Flight* golf balls but change my mind. I slip a fifty-dollar bill from my wallet ...

When I hear yelling from the cell next to me, I jolt to a sitting position. Minutes later the small opening in my door flings open and a guard pushes through a bowl of tomato soup and a hunk of bread. I feel hunger pangs and know I must eat. Otherwise, I'll lose more weight and become weaker.

I approach the first tee. My golf bag sits on the back of the electric cart. I pull out my driver and put the tee into the ground, pushing hard, as the dirt is dry. I take the golf ball from my pocket and roll it around in my hands before I set it on the tee. I take several practice swings, study the terrain, and line up my shot with the flag and...

I hear a man sobbing and look out my meal slot. Two guards, both sweaty musclemen, come to the cell across from me to transport my neighbor to Jackson prison. "I won't go," he screams. "You set me up." His distress makes me panic. I pace back and forth in my cell.

To prevent myself from losing control, I turn myself into a golf ball. Whack! My driver thwacks me. I fly through the air. The hard wallops, the ones that hurt the most, are long drives, 250 yards or more. Sometimes, there's a light hit, a chip shot. The sand trap. Dammit. I hate sand traps. Another thwack. I soar from the trap. I give myself over to the man's situation, to golf, to futility. The guards finally leave with my cell neighbor in restraints.

I'm on the green now, line my ball up with the flag, and decide the best way to play the break. At thirty feet away, I'll be lucky if I make it. I tap the ball. It rolls; it's going in, a one putt. At the last minute, the ball turns and stops three feet from the hole. I tap the ball in for a two putt. I bend over the hole to retrieve my golf ball, walk off the green, then put the putter back in my golf bag and drive my cart to the second hole…

Another day a guard tells me a prisoner has had a heart attack and died. "Sometimes the prisoners get out of control with a death," he says. 'We watch everyone in nearby cells for twenty-four hours." He walks up and down the corridor looking for unusual behavior.

I'm pacing in my cell as I approach the third hole. It's a long one, 510 yards, with a football stadium sized pond in front of it filled with blue-green water and lily pads. Large sand traps are positioned on each side. I need to lay up my shot to get over the water, but first I must get a long drive…

I swing my driver and hit the ball squarely. It soars. I close my eyes, then open them for a second. My ball lands in the middle of the fairway, a good shot, 200 yards. I pick up my three wood and swing again. Another good shot. I'm right in front of the lake. I choose my seven iron as the best club to get over the water.

I force myself to finish my game, then lie on my cot and fall asleep.

I play golf every day, eighteen holes, sometimes twenty-seven. I'm always alone on the course like I'm alone here, solitary confinement.

I'm fed three meals a day and force myself to eat some of the institutional fare, not even close to Mom's home cooking. Every day, they give me a basin of water to wash with. I keep myself as clean as possible.

I find a pebble and hide it in the corner of my cell to scratch small lines in the cement floor to keep track of the days. I figure ten weeks have passed. My golf game gets better every week. I ask the pimply guard, who sometimes is friendly, to give me a piece of chalk. He brings a stub the next day, and I keep score. I never shoot below par.

Frank Holloway tells me the date of my trial is January 5th. That morning the guards take me to the courthouse. The chains they wrap around my ankles make me shuffle as I walk along. My attorney suggests I waive a jury trial to make it easier to focus on the evidence of my case. A bench trial, where a judge decides my fate, is also quicker and less expensive.

Dad and Mike are sitting in the visitor's section. Tears run down my cheeks when I see them. I'm not required to testify. I only state my name, "Daniel Maling, birth date June 24, 1999."

Frank Holloway presents a compelling case for self-defense. He brings in witnesses to prove Alicia's story is fabricated. She and her friends set the entire scenario up, figuring that I'd give her male friend my wallet and walk away. She must have seen the bills in my wallet when I paid for our drinks.

Alicia is made accessory to a crime. I am free. I lean back in my chair, overcome with such strong emotion, that I cannot speak. I take deep breaths and stand up when Dad and Mike come to embrace me. "We knew you were innocent all along," Dad says.

Mike grins, "We just called Mom to let her know the good news."

***

Later in the day, I'm released. A guard escorts me to another section of the jail. He hands me a brown paper bag with my old clothes. I change into my jeans and button-down shirt. I feel like a new man. Wearing regular shoes makes all the difference.

I walk out the door and breathe in the frigid January air. Dad and Mike are waiting. Mike hands me my old L.L Bean jacket. We embrace. "We're going home and not letting you out of our sight for weeks," he says.

Sitting in the car's passenger seat, I relax and lean my head back. I tell them how I played golf every day in my head, how I visualized the course, the shots, all of it.

Mike, who is driving, looks over at me. "You know, Dude, researchers have found that playing any sport in your head every day for several weeks improves your real game."

I smile. "Never knew that, but we'll have to find out if it's true one of these days."

We pass through my old neighborhood. My hands shake and my heart pounds. I feel as if I will explode—a panic attack. I unfasten my seat belt and try to get up. "Help. I have to get out," I scream. Mike pulls the car over onto a side street. The two of us pace up and down the sidewalk. Soon I am calm again. Then, I start to bawl like a baby.

Dad and Mom insist I come home, stay with them for a while. They hire a physical therapist who sees me three times a week. I grow stronger and have more energy but refuse to talk about the hard times I had in jail. Forcing myself to forget keeps the wolf at bay. I'm tense and fear that someone will jump me anytime I leave the house. I refuse Mike's suggestion to get out on the golf course but play every day in my head.

Mike suggests I see a counselor. I refuse even though I'm depressed and moody, flying off the handle at any little problem. "I'm not a wimp," I tell him.

The evenings are hard. I have trouble sleeping. I struggle to figure out why I had to endure these months of agony. One night, I wake up screaming and find myself under the bed knocking my head against the slats. Dad rushes in.

"A nightmare," I say once I settle down. "Not to worry."

Days later Mike moves in. He sleeps in the twin bed beside me. Anytime I wake up screaming, he holds me until the terrifying images disappear. Some days I have trouble controlling in my anger. I almost strangle a neighbor's barking dog but fortunately stop before I hurt the animal or anyone sees me.

***

When I knock out the jackass pushing ahead of me in the 7-Eleven cashier's line, the manager calls the cops. To avoid an assault and battery charge, I agree to be hospitalized in an inpatient psychiatric unit.

The nurses there are kind. I join support group discussions with other nut cases like myself, two of them ex-jailbirds like me. The nurse leading the group encourages me to talk. Once I start describing my experiences, I can't stop.

I tell them and my psychologist how I played golf every day in my head and how it helped me get through the long days spent in solitary confinement. Everyone listens; they care. The psychologist explains how my experiences in jail have traumatized me so badly that I now suffer from Post Traumatic Stress Disorder. He encourages me to follow my dream of becoming a golf pro.

In two months, my nightmares and panic attacks ease. I feel calmer on the inside, healed, and ready to go home.

***

"Let's play golf," my brother suggests several days after I'm discharged. I agree. We go to my favorite course, the one in Traverse City. We rent an electric cart and drive to the first hole.

"You're up first," Mike says.

Can I still play well, shoot par? Even though I know the course by heart, like the lines in the palm of my hand, I'm unsure.

I plan my game carefully, just as I did in jail. My hands shake when I pick up my old driver. I tighten my grip, and the shaking stops. I swing. I hit the ball. It soars high in the sky, at least 200 yards down the middle of the fairway.

I shoot two strokes under par, the best game I've ever played. I feel like a hero. As I walk off the eighteenth hole, I raise my club in the air and shake it. "You were right. My golf game has improved."

Mike puts his arm around my shoulder. "You haven't lost your touch. I'm excited for you."

"It's great to be out here with you again. You know I'll always love golf. It saved my life, but I have some news. I've decided not to be a golf pro anymore. I've given it a lot of thought. I'm gonna be a nurse, a psych nurse, so I can help other guys and gals who need support getting their heads together. I can always play golf on the side."

Mike stares at me, his mouth agape.

"Those nurses in the psych hospital worked like dogs, but they cared and understood us in a way no one else could. Every patient has a story. Hearing all of theirs helped me talk about mine."

"You, a nurse?" Mike's eyes open wide. His jaws drop. "I can't believe it."

"Yeah, a nurse like you."

"God, Bro. You must have developed your ESP skills in the clinker. Since you've been home, I've laid awake so many nights thinking about how I can help the men and women who are broken and self-medicate with street drugs and booze. I see them in the ER all the time, but I don't have time to know what's been going on in their heads. We send them out. Two weeks later they're back in. Anyhow, I've changed my specialty to psych, all because of you. I start my in-service next week. You've inspired me big time."

My eyes tear. I smile. Mike leans toward me and says, "Nurse to nurse." We embrace in a long bear hug.

I Don't Want Another Mother

I sat on the edge of the exam table waiting for Dr. Reynolds to speak. The serious look in his eyes alerted me that something was seriously wrong. "Melanie, your cervix is thinning, and you're only six months along."

When I put my hand over my abdomen, I was rewarded with two quick baby kicks. "But it should be okay, right? I feel good and still work three evenings a week at the hospital." Because of my big belly, my scrubs now were an extra-large. I didn't tell him how slow I walked up and down the unit's hallways. Nor did I tell him how Justin and I needed the money I earned to cover our household expenses. Working evenings when my husband was home meant we didn't need a babysitter for our three-year-old.

Since I'd been a psych nurse for the last ten years, my knowledge of high-risk pregnancies was obsolete. I searched my brain for the implications of Dr. Reynolds' words. The seconds of silence seemed to span an eternity.

He fingered the pen in his lab coat pocket. "The ultrasound shows the twins are developing normally, but they're still too small to survive on their own. I'm writing you a script for steroids, which will help the babies' lungs mature."

"So will they survive if they're born early?" I braced my arms on the sides of the examining table, both wanting to hear his answer yet fearing it.

"There's a better chance, but the longer we can hold off, the stronger they'll be. I'm very concerned about premature labor in the next month. I'd like you to quit work now, and we'll schedule ultrasounds every couple weeks to keep an eye on them."

I covered my face with my hands. "Oh my God, I could lose my babies after all this."

My breath quickened. Flashes of my nursing school days working in the neonatal ICU shot through my mind. The infants lying in the clear plastic isolettes almost always needed IV therapy. Many were attached to monitors and some even needed ventilators to breathe for them. I remembered the strained looks on the parents' faces and their constant fear that their children would die or be mentally or physically challenged. Back then I never imagined that one day I would be in the same situation. My mouth went dry.

He shook his head. "We'll do our best to keep labor from starting. From now on, I want you to spend most of the day in bed to keep the pressure off your uterus. Only get up to go to the bathroom and to shower."

"But what about our son, Evan? He's only three and won't understand why I can't play with him."

"What about his dad? Can he take some time off work? There's family leave, you know."

I twirled my wedding ring around my finger. "Now that it's tax season, Justin can be on the computer 'til ten or eleven at night except for the days I work when he watches him alone." I paused. "I guess that's a done deal."

I waited for Dr. Reynolds to smile, but he didn't. Instead he said, "This might be the time to get family and friends involved. We'll order you a hospital bed but only elevate the back to fifteen or so degrees to keep the pressure off your cervix. You'll be more comfortable in the hospital bed, and you can put it in a main part of the house but sleep in your regular bed with your head on two pillows at night."

Tears came to my eyes. While Justin and I hadn't planned on the pregnancy, we weren't disappointed, but we were shocked to be having twins. Neither of our families had a history of multiple births. "I want these babies to be healthy, but I have to think this through. It's not as easy as you make it sound." I ran my fingers through my hair.

"Melanie, you can drive home this afternoon, but then arrange to get help. This is serious. My nurse will phone you tomorrow to make sure everything is coordinated."

I left Dr. Reynolds office in a daze. Sitting in my SUV, I phoned Justin. I wiped tears and choked back sobs as I told him the news.

His voice cracked. "Stay where you are and keep calm. I'm coming to drive you home. Your uncle and I will pick up the SUV later. We'll work this out."

Justin's words reassured me. A half hour later I sat in the front seat of his Altima. His hand resting on my leg comforted me. I wanted to stay in the passenger seat forever, looking out the side window to see dusk settling down over the highway outside of Boston as people headed home at the end of their workday. Daydreaming about others' lives was easier than dealing with my own.

Justin eased the car to a stop at a red light and squeezed my hand. His forehead had those lines across it, the ones that meant there was a problem. "I called your aunt a bit ago to see if she could help. More bad news. She slipped on the ice this morning and has been in the ER since one this afternoon. She has a bad sprain, probably tore some ligaments in her ankle plus she has a gash on her hand that needed several stitches. She sounded a bit confused."

I felt the blood drain from my face. "Aunt Jennifer, hurt. She's always so careful. She should have known better than to be outside when the weather is bad." My aunt was like a mother to me. Always smiling and rarely complaining, she made my world a safe place.

My real mother cared more about her banking career than her children and made benign inattentiveness her parenting credo. She was always too busy to hug Brian and me or listen to our little problems. Like her response the time my date for the sophomore prom dumped me at the last minute—'Don't waste your tears.' When I was sixteen, I started calling her Alice, and she didn't even ask why.

Aunt Jennifer, Alice's older sister had no children of her own. In spite of her part-time work at the crisis center, she was always happy to drive me to cheerleading practice, my math tutor, and ice skating-lessons. She became the mother I always wanted. I adored her—her endless love, her warm laugh, and her impulsive unpredictable behavior. Her husband, Uncle Ned, was a kind and quiet man who spent most of his spare time in their garage working on old Model Ts.

Justin paused. "It was black ice; Jen didn't see it. She feels terrible this happened today. She thinks she can help us in two or three weeks and doesn't want you to worry. I have everything covered for today. Uncle Ned will pick up Evan at day care on his way home from work and meet us at the house. I ordered a pizza and an antipasto salad to be delivered for dinner. After we eat, he'll go with me to get our SUV."

My thoughts circled my head like goldfish swimming in a small bowl. "What are we going to do?"

"We need to call your mother."

My heart skipped a beat. "But Alice hardly knows Evan." After my parents' divorce and her move to Tucson, we rarely saw her as she insisted visiting once a year was 'adequate.'

Justin sighed. "She's our best choice. We have to try and pray she'll agree. We can't afford to pay a fulltime sitter for even two or three weeks. She'll learn Evan's routine in a day or two, and you'll be there to supervise."

"You're right, but dammit. Alice ties me up in knots when we're together. And she can be bossy."

Over the years my mother and I learned to respect each other and keep our peace, but we didn't have much in common. Conversations were stiff; her black and white way at looking at life bored me as much as my interest in people and their relationships bored her. I felt stupid and incompetent around her; I almost felt I'd been born into the wrong family.

"Just for a couple weeks 'til we can figure out something else. Jennifer thinks she'll be okay by then."

Tears ran down my cheeks. "I wish Jen could help us now. She's great with Evan, and he adores her."

Justin took a deep breath. "We can offer to fly Alice here; there's a direct flight from Tucson to Boston. Just 'til we make other plans. Jennifer has a life now, too, so we can't depend on her entirely. Even though she's retired from the crisis center, she is involved with all those charities. It would be great if Alice could stay on longer and alternate days with Jen. We'd save a lot of money."

"I feel bad to still need Jen." I sighed and wiped my eyes. "All right. I'll check with Alice and hope she can come 'til we can make other plans."

Justin pulled the Altima into the driveway. "I already called her, and she agreed."

I wanted to punch him but forced myself to stay calm. After all, she was my mother. "Okay," I muttered. "At least we're set for a couple weeks." I got out of the car, slammed the door, and walked into the house.

Evan sat in his booster chair eating pizza with Uncle Ned. When my son saw me, he set down his sippy cup and waved his arms. "Mommy home."

Ned stood up to hug me. "Have to get back to the hospital to pick up Jen. She texted me twenty minutes ago but insisted I stay 'til you two got home from the doctors." Once Ned left, I kissed my son's tomatoey face, rumpled his hair, and then sat down to eat.

When we finished, Justin took my arm and led me to the bedroom. "You need to rest, Sweetheart. Tomorrow the hospital bed should be here."

He was right. Soon, I fell into a restless sleep but awakened several times with Dr. Reynolds' warning replaying in my mind. In the morning, I opened my eyes to find Justin's arm looped around my shoulder.

I laid my head on his chest. "Amazing how everything came together so easily. You've organized all this and kept your cheerful attitude. I owe you."

He kissed me on the forehead. "It will be a while, but I'll take the rain check."

"Probably a month or so after the twins are born." I rubbed my stomach. "These babies are lucky. They will have a good dad."

Carefully tucking the blanket in around my neck, Justin ran his fingers through my auburn bedhead hair. "Alice's flying in this afternoon to help us. I'm taking the day off work and will pick her up at the airport at four. She sounded pleased to be asked, paid extra to buy her ticket at the last minute."

I sighed. "All right, but why did this have to happen? I was just getting used to the idea of twins and now this complication of needing help. It's not fair."

"Who knows, Melanie? Things happen. We don't know why."

I fluffed up my pillow. "Two or three months are a long time. I'm scared I'll go crazy with worry. I could lose the babies or they could be born handicapped. And Alice being here will make it worse. She makes me feel so incompetent I can't even be my normal self when I'm around her." My voice choked.

"Let's just take it one day at a time. Don't anticipate problems. Right now, I'm going to the kitchen. You'll be the queen for the day. I'll serve you breakfast in bed."

When he came back with oatmeal, orange juice, and a bagel lathered with peanut butter for the two of us, I forced a smile. By the time we'd finished eating, I'd faced reality and my plan to deal with Alice was in place. I would use the same guidelines I had taught many of my patients who struggled with dysfunctional relationships.

Talk about your emotions. Let others know what you are feeling at the time you're feeling it; don't let resentments fester. Say what you want from others and why. Listen to the other's point of view without interrupting. Compliment appropriately. Find commonalities. Laugh and use subtle humor. Would these techniques work with Alice? I wasn't sure. Would I be able to do my part? These strategies were more difficult to enact than they sounded.

I remembered the many times Jennifer babysat for my brother and me when we were in grade school. She'd arranged her work schedule to be free after 2:30 many afternoons. I loved coming home from school and finding a plate of chocolate chip cookies and a glass of milk on the kitchen table. It would be so much easier if Alice treated me like Jen. Even though my aunt worked part-time at the crisis center before she retired, she acted as if my brother and I were her own children.

She cooked our favorite foods, planned great holiday get-togethers, and bought us little presents just for the heck of it. She even taught me how to blow dry my hair.

When I was in high school, she took me to help with the crisis center's homeless shelter. At first, talking to the people needing assistance for food and clothes scared me. I wasn't used to people who looked unkempt and dressed in tattered clothes. Yet I smiled at them and learned it was easy to get them talking by asking a few basic questions and, with Jen's direction, built a few ongoing relationships. The difficulties the mentally ill faced particularly interested me. I attributed my interest in psychology and psychiatric nursing to her and the people she served.

For parties and family get-togethers, Jennifer dressed stylishly. At the shelter, she wore basic clothes. "It's important to blend in with your clientele," she told me. With everyone though, she shared her warm, loving smile, spontaneous hugs, new age philosophy, and soft humor. I laughed when I was around her in spite of her scatterbrained and melodramatic tendencies.

Alice must have grown up on another planet. She liked comfortable clothes and didn't enjoy shopping, going to the spa, or checking out new model homes. Now that she'd retired, she filled the hours of her day following the stock market and even doing some day trading. She liked to read mysteries or be outside gardening, walking, or bike riding. Unlike Jen, she has no interest in self-help books or working with poor people.

Alice never agreed to a babysitting trip until now. She might have watched Evan for an evening when she visited for the holidays, but she didn't seem to need us to make her happy. She preferred the warm Arizona sun to the snowy winters of Boston. I didn't know why she was willing to come now

Right after Justin and I married, she asked me to please stop calling her Alice. She said we should act more like a normal family, that it needed to change before the grandchildren came. I agreed at the time, but saying *Mom* never felt right. I found all kinds of ways to skirt the issue, like looking directly at her when asking a question. I called her Nana if I was forced to identify her in a conversation, but each time she told me she was not my grandmother.

We both couldn't escape the truth. Jennifer was my mother, and now Alice and I were stuck with each other 24/7.

***

Three days later, I lay in my hospital bed in the family room talking on my cell to my nurse manager, Kelly, and low enough so Alice wouldn't hear me. "Yes, she's here. She tries to help but she's driving me crazy. She's useless in the kitchen. I have to explain how to use the microwave, coffee bean grinder, and food processor—not once, twice, but three or four times. She spilled coffee all over the floor and on her tennis shoes this morning. She's so awkward."

Alice was loading the dishwasher after making us pancakes for breakfast. Her pink shell necklace clanked against the sink. Oblivious to me on the phone, she said, "Do you think Evan watches too much television? There are a lot of other things he could be doing."

I said a quick good-bye to Kelly. When I looked at my mother's short curly perm, dyed a light brown, and her aqua blue slack outfit, I gritted my teeth once again. Taking a deep breath, I counted the days until Jennifer could take over. "Evan has his shows, some educational. His pre-school teacher recommends the kids watch several of them. It's a break for me too."

She frowned. "Just a thought, Melanie."

One afternoon Alice took Evan to the park to play. I didn't like that he came home with his jeans covered with dirt. Another time, she let Evan drink out of her water bottle. Didn't she know about germs? I'd spent hours teaching him not to drink after others. Thank God he was toilet trained; Alice didn't need to get involved with that.

I hadn't told her my plans to go back to college and earn my MBA, so I could move into a nurse manager position at the hospital once the children were in school. I didn't talk about it much to others either, fearing I would end up parenting my children the way Alice mothered me. Now with the twins coming, my career plans would be on hold for a while. I loved my job, yet the next few years could be the perfect opportunity to be a stay-at-home mother and personally raise my kids, not be like Alice and let someone else do it. Once Justin and I talked about having children, I resolved to be different than my mother, which is why I worked evenings when Justin could watch Evan.

I was scared I wouldn't have the patience for full time mothering. The ultrasound showed that the twins were boys; parenting three children 24/7—how would I do it? Even with his morning pre-school, taking care of Evan had been difficult.

After Alice finished cleaning up the kitchen, she brought me a cup of tea with sugar and lemon just the way I liked it. Justin must have told her to do that. She never would have figured it out by herself. "Thank you," I said.

Evan watched *Thomas and Friends* on television while he waited for the carpool driver to pick him up for day care. When the horn beeped, Alice held him up so he could hug me good-bye.

"Love you, Mommy," he whispered.

I watched him walk out the door and realized it would be a long time before I could lift him myself. "Bye, Sweetheart," I said even though it felt as if there were a balloon in my throat. When Alice pulled a chair next to the bed, I sighed and forced myself to smile. "Thanks for making breakfast."

"You're welcome. I'll find something special to do with Evan after pre-school," she told me. "Maybe I'll take him outside. It's a little nippy, so I'll make sure he stays out of the dirt and wears a scarf and mittens. He might get a cold if he gets chilled."

I set my empty teacup on my bedside table. "Great to keep him warm but that won't keep him from getting sick."

"I raised you and your brother, and you're both healthy," Alice said.

"I spent three years in nursing school. Colds come from viruses, not from being outside in inclement weather."

A frown replaced her smile. "Whatever," she said, turning away.

The doorbell rang. I hoped it was Jen; I couldn't wait to see her.

Alice got up to answer the door. "Jennifer, good to see you, but what a surprise. I'm sorry about your fall." Her voice sounded more high-pitched than usual. "How did you get here?"

"An Uber. Aren't they wonderful?" Jen hobbled in and hung her Michael Kors purse on the doorknob. "Yesterday, of all the days to slip on the ice. Dammit. Here I only live ten minutes away and you had to come all the way from Arizona to help out."

"The least I can do for the kids," Alice said. "This is a good chance for me to reconnect. I've been missing them."

"I'm supposed to stay in and keep my leg up, but being here now is more important than being at home." Her face looked haggard and pale.

Muttering "I came all the way here for this," Alice turned and walked to the kitchen. Fortunately, Jennifer was looking the other way and didn't hear her.

Tears of relief welled up in my eyes. Aunt Jennifer here. Maybe I could finally relax. Yet she wasn't acting quite like her old self. She certainly wasn't in any shape to watch Evan.

Still wearing her brown leather coat, Jennifer shuffled over to the bed and hugged me. Her left foot was in an immobilizer, and an Ace bandage was wrapped around her right hand. "Melanie, I had to come to help. Oh you poor thing. I couldn't stop thinking about you. Being here with you will help me feel better."

She casually tossed her coat and cashmere scarf on the sofa. Then, she sat down in the recliner in the corner of the room and elevated her legs. "This chair is wonderful. Keeps my foot up just like the doctor wanted."

I'd never seen my aunt look so bleak. "Aunt Jen, you look tired. Really beat. Have you been sleeping?"

"How can I sleep knowing what you are going through? And my new grand nephews. What if we lose them? I couldn't bear it." Her voice choked.

My aunt's comments filled me with anxiety. I clenched my fists to keep my hands from shaking. She was echoing my deepest fear.

Alice cleared her throat. "We're taking it one day at a time, Jennifer. Dr. Reynolds is hopeful, and so am I. You should be too."

To my surprise, Alice's no-nonsense practical approach comforted me, and I wondered how long it had been since something she did made me feel better. Perhaps once I'd married and had Evan, I'd never given her the opportunity.

Jennifer adjusted her leg on the chair and winced. "Alice, would you mind getting my Tramadol out of my handbag and bringing me a glass of water. My ankle's throbbing."

"Not at all," Alice said.

My aunt's hands shook as she swallowed her pill. "How's my little Evan? I want him to have brothers. What if the babies are born handicapped? Lying alone in those hospital incubators with tubes stuck in their little bodies. Have you been eating right, Melanie? What about Justin?"

The flicker of concern that crossed Alice's face felt like the same one tearing through my heart. How could Jennifer say such terrible things? I realized how few times my aunt had had to deal with a family health problem. It was Alice who stepped up to be Granny's caregiver when she had pneumonia.

A gust of fear swept through me like the winter wind blowing through the Boston Harbor. I forced myself to keep my voice even. "It's hard being in bed, Jen, but I'm doing okay. Justin and Evan are fine, too."

"But Sweetie, I feel so useless. Out of the loop. The doctor told me to stay home for a week but I had to come. I've been a wreck sitting around the house. I can't drive for three more weeks, so I won't be able to get back to my volunteering either."

I raised the head of my hospital bed. "Jen, you have to take care of yourself. Either go home and rest or go to the bedroom and lie down. You're making me nervous. Does Uncle Ned know you're here?"

"No. He didn't want me to come, but he's at work so…"

Jennifer was funny and witty most of the time, even the life of the party when things were going well, but now her emotions were taking over. She was in no shape to help us. How selfish I had been to expect that. Now with this pregnancy, I couldn't even help my favorite aunt.

I lowered the head of my hospital bed, then reached for my cell phone. "Let me call Uncle Ned for you."

"Oh Melanie. I feel so bad. I want to stay, but you're right. I need to go home and rest. Call him for me, please."

Noticing my distress, Alice interrupted us. "I'll make the phone call. And, Jennifer, let me help you to the other recliner in the den. Melanie needs to rest."

Relieved that someone else was handling the problem, I handed Alice the cell phone. I hadn't realized how tired I was.

Twenty minutes later, Uncle Ned was at the door, upset that Jennifer had gone out by herself. "I'll take her right home," he said as he hugged me good-bye. He acted calm and reassuring as he escorted her out the door.

After Jennifer's visit, my stomach churned and an acidy taste filled my mouth. Maybe it wasn't such a bad idea that Alice was here. I realized my aunt was great for the day-to day fun activities but not so good when things got tough. Right at that moment, I decided to not take advantage of Jen's good nature any longer.

Alice walked over and sat at the foot of my bed. When she took my hand, I broke out in tears. "Thanks for helping out with Jennifer," I mumbled. "I'm really scared. The babies could be born early, and preemies need a lot of care. Jen doesn't often act like that. She freaked me out."

"It could be the pain. She's also worried about you and herself. You're strong, and you're taking good care of yourself. We have to stay positive."

"I've not had any contractions, and there's medicine to stop them if I do. The babies should be big enough to survive in another month."

"It's not that long, Melanie. We can do this together."

"I don't know if I can do it, raise three children. I mean—I love Evan but being with him for hours on end tires me out. And then to have two more."

She handed me a tissue. "Believe it or not, I remember. I was exhausted for months after both Brian and you were born. Somehow, I got through. No one tells you that playing with kids all day can be tiring and boring. I had to go back to work to keep my sanity. I struggled for months before making my decision."

"Yeah, but it hurt us not having you there. Even when you were home, your mind was always ten million miles away. I missed you."

"I'm sorry if I left you kids adrift and didn't give you enough attention. I didn't mean to hurt you. I wanted you to learn to be independent and able to take care of yourselves. I didn't know you were unhappy. You never complained."

I wiped away a tear. "I didn't understand my childhood could have been different. I accepted my life for what it was and kept on smiling."

"I understand that now. I didn't see my mistakes until I retired and listened to other women's stories about their families, until it was too late." She sighed. "I'm trying to play with Evan the way I should have played with you, but I did keep a clean house and made sure you had breakfast and did your homework and went to bed on time."

"But Jen and my friends' moms were fun to be around." I paused to collect my thoughts. "You seemed to be lost in your own world. I wasn't sure you loved me."

"Oh, Melanie. It tears me up to hear you say that. I've always loved you." She put her arms around me and murmured, "I hope we can start over."

Sensing her sincerity, I took a deep breath and said, "We can sure try."

"Being here has opened up a whole new world for me. I need to change and be more involved in your life and with Brian's family, too. So many important things I've put on the back burner." She bit her lip.

I pondered her words. "Our family problems didn't matter so much to Brian when we were growing up. He's a happily married man and seems like an involved dad. I hate that he lives in Hawaii. It's so far away. We text each other every so often."

She nodded. "We connect every few weeks on FaceTime. He's always pleasant. He and Sally bring the kids to visit every couple years, but they never have invited me over."

I squeezed her hand. "Maybe he's afraid you'll say 'yes' to the trip. Who knows?"

She laughed. "You could be right. Maybe we can FaceTime him while I'm here."

"Good idea, but let's chat more later. Right now I'm tired and need a break." My mind whirled with confusion. What had gotten into Alice? She was acting different, almost like a real person with feelings. She'd given me a lot to think about.

"I understand." She looked down and pulled a loose thread from her sweater.

I inched my legs over the side of the bed. "I'm going to take a shower and wash my hair. Relax; work your crossword or check out one of the magazines on the coffee table."

Alice looked at her watch. "Evan's driver should be dropping him off in ten minutes or so."

"Yeah, you're right. He can watch a DVD. Remember how to put it in?"

"Justin wrote out the directions. Take it easy in there. Call me if you need anything."

"Thanks. I should be okay."

While I was in the bathroom, I heard the answering machine pick up a call, hopefully not an important one. When I came back into the family room, Alice was on the floor building blocks with Evan. I flipped on the voice mail and found a message from the admission's counselor at the college telling me about a schedule change for my first class. As I eased myself back into my bed, I felt Alice's eyes boring down on me. I realized she'd listened to the message earlier. By mistake, I must have listed our home phone on the admissions form.

"I didn't realize you were going back to school," she said as she slowly stood up and then sat on the sofa.

Miraculously, Evan continued to build a block tower by himself. He was already up to six blocks and it still hadn't fallen. A surprise to me as I hadn't played blocks with him in weeks. Maybe I'd been too wrapped up in work or too pregnant to get down on my hands and knees with him; and here Alice was sitting on the floor, getting up and down probably with arthritis or a ligament problem. Her knee had clicked when she stood up earlier. What had I been thinking? Evan really had warmed up to Alice; playing with her had been good for him. How many times had I scolded him, 'Not now. I have to get ready for work.' Was I parenting like Alice and not realizing it?

I rearranged my pillows. "I admit I find mothering to be challenging and requires skills I don't have. I wish I felt different. I love Evan to pieces, but his always needing something drives me crazy. At home, I feel as if I have lost my identity."

"Being a mother is hard work. Just when you have one problem solved, another pops up. I understand all that. Most mothers feel pulled in many different directions." The furrows around the corners of her eyes deepened. Perhaps, she was thinking of her early mothering years.

"Maybe I'm not cut out for it as much as I thought. Working in the hospital is important to me, and Evan likes day care, so it feels like a win-win. Maybe I'm more like you than I think."

Alice smiled. "You're ten steps ahead of where I was at your age. What are you thinking?"

"I need an MBA to become a nurse manager; administration is my forte. My classes start in September, part time. Justin agreed to get home from work a little early to babysit."

"Isn't tuition expensive?"

I nodded. "Horribly, we're taking out a home equity loan, and I'll work overtime some week-end evenings once the babies get older."

"Oh, Melanie." She sighed. "You remind me so much of myself when I was your age. I wanted it all, nice home, career, achieving kids, satisfying marriage, and I worked hard to get it. You know some of the story, how Dad's father moved in with us after his stroke and lived in our back bedroom for two years. Hospice and I took care of him before he died. Do you remember how I took care of Granny even though she didn't live with us?"

"I vaguely remember. That must have been a big change for you. I never gave your personal life much thought 'til now." And to think I was a psych nurse yet unable to work through my childhood issues.

"Because I never talked about it, you don't know the early stuff. How Dad and I almost got a divorce two years after we married because I wanted to go to law school so badly. I even contacted an attorney to start the paperwork, because Dad threatened to put me on a restricted allowance. Can you imagine the humiliation?"

"No, I'd never stand for that."

"I guess it worked out as life tends to do whether we like it or not. Dad and I ended up compromising. I got the bank teller job, forgot about law school, and worked my way up to a manager. Our relationship was flat, stale as a slice of dried bread, but I stayed for you kids and my own comfort until I couldn't stand it anymore. That's what women did back then. It's different now. The rules have changed. You have many more options."

"Yeah, the options are there for our generation, once we figure out which ones we want."

I looked at the faraway expression in Alice's eyes and took her hand. "I guess I knew you weren't happy but never understood why."

"Work was my outlet. That and my friends at the bank kept me sane."

She ran her thumb over my fingers. "I have a little extra money now from Social Security and my investments. It's important to follow your dreams. I'd like to pay for your first semester. We'll see how it goes after that. I'd hate to see you and Justin under pressure to pay off a home equity loan."

Tears came to my eyes. My anger and hurt had disappeared.

Alice wiped my face with a tissue. "You know, I can plan to come for a month or so in the summer to help you out. This trip has made me see that I can fit in with you, Justin, and the kids."

"That's pretty special. Thank you, Mom." I swallowed hard.

I took a deep breath. How fast my relationship with my mother had changed. How wrong I was about her and about myself. How judgmental and uncaring I had been. Our changed relationship was all because my personal crisis forced us to share our feelings.

***

I really do need another mother. In fact, I'll take as many mothers as I can get, especially if they're like the two I already have.

Summer at Sunnybrook Farm

"Nurse Debbie, Nurse Debbie," Hannah screamed as I pulled into Sunnybrook Camp's parking lot. For three years, she'd attended the camp's month-long summer program. Hannah, a high functioning Downs child, was a chubby thirteen-year-old with poker-straight brown hair and hazel eyes. She rushed over to hug me as I stepped out of my car. "I missed you all winter," she exclaimed. "I love my camp." She patted her chest. "It's one of the suns that lives inside my heart."

What a welcome! Memories of my past three summers here drifted through my mind like gliding down a lazy river in an inner tube. "I missed you, too, Hannah." I placed my hands on her shoulders. "How much you've grown." I was always fascinated to see the changes in her and some of the other kids from year to year.

Sunnybrook Camp, a small camp set in northeastern Pennsylvania's Pocono Mountains, was snuggled in among lush maple, cedar, and hemlock trees. The camp integrated children with special needs with those considered *normal*. Most kids spent part of each day either swimming, kayaking, or rafting in the clear but cold lake water. I'd grown to love this place with its twenty ramshackle cabins and the mess hall with its beat-up wooden benches and long rectangular tables. As the camp nurse, my job was to provide emergency and routine health care to the fifty campers and twenty counselors. Treating minor injuries and illnesses, monitoring chronic conditions like diabetes and epilepsy, and triaging any serious problems were the crux of my job description.

The staff all worked together to expose the kids to outdoor living, teach them to look after themselves, get along with others, and accept their differences. Some campers, especially the city kids, never spent much time in the great outdoors or away from their families. Many would return home a different person than when they left.

Hannah followed me to my small bedroom in the back of the infirmary. She chatted about the fun morning she'd had rafting with Brian, a thirteen-year-old cancer survivor, who'd spent his last three summers at the camp. While I organized my clothes in the wooden dresser, Hannah wiped down the round kitchen table and three chairs with Pine Sol several times over.

Finally, she laid down the rag. "You're taking too long, Nurse Debbie. Come on. We need to walk around and see everybody."

"Once I get the sheets on the bed, we can go." Last year I would have been annoyed with Hannah's willfulness, but today I found it endearing.

She ran to the bathroom closet and brought back the linens. I pulled the twin bed in the corner away from the wall. She helped me tuck the sheets and blanket under the mattress, then sat down on the quilted spread and said, "We made your room beautiful, like the sun."

"We sure did. You helped me a lot, Hannah." I smiled, brushed my long auburn hair, and pinned my name tag, Deborah Adams RN, on my t-shirt. Hannah's sun was something I wish I had

Arm in arm, we walked down the hall to the infirmary, which were three rooms connected to each other—a waiting room with four plastic chairs, an exam room with a table and desk, and a separate room with three cots for overnight patients. Later this evening, I would organize the children's charts, check that the parents had completed the health questionnaires, and acquaint myself with the kid's medications and any treatment protocols.

First, Hannah dragged me to the kitchen connected to the mess hall. "See, Nurse Debbie, not much has changed from last year."

Hannah spotted Sarah, a kitchen helper who sat behind a table icing sugar cookies in the room's far corner, and rushed toward her. She stood in front of Sarah for several moments, waiting patiently until she handed both of us broken cookies to sample.

We sat down at a small nearby table. I accepted a Styrofoam cup of coffee from a twenty-some year-old guy, probably about my age, whom I'd never met before. He had a scruffy beard and an owl tattoo on his right forearm and walked with a slight limp. I wondered why. An unruly cowlick on the back of his head gave him a nerdy look, but his blue eyes and gentle smile made the limp and cowlick irrelevant.

"Welcome to Sunnybrook," he said "You look like the upbeat nurse the staff has been expecting. My name's Bono, by the way. Maybe we can talk later. I need to get back to the kitchen and the sloppy joes I'm making for lunch."

Bono. For a few seconds I wondered why anyone would choose such an unusual name, then decided it wasn't any of my business.

Once we finished our cookies, Hannah ran off to join a group of campers in the arts and crafts area. Minutes later, Todd, a counselor I'd worked with last summer but who had ignored the texts and emails I'd sent over the winter, sat down beside me. I thought I'd forgotten him, but my heart quickened remembering the times we'd spent together in his cabin after our weekend parties, several overnights I enjoyed at the time in spite of the camp's NO SEX rule.

"Hey Debs. Good to see you." Todd winked and wrapped me in a bear hug. "Hope we can start over where we left off last July. Meant to answer your texts but got too busy."

God, how much of a player could this guy be? I took a deep breath and pulled away, vowing not to fall into this boyfriend trap again and to keep my relationship with the male staff professional. I needed someone solid, someone I could trust, not a guy I connected with for a month in a summer camp.

"I'm not going to party this summer, Todd. I've got plenty to do in the evenings texting my boyfriend." That wasn't the first lie I'd ever told in my life.

He shrugged and walked away.

Fate was not in my corner. Todd and I were often paired together with our student groups of eight boys and eight girls. We even ate at the same long table in the mess hall. One day as we were wiping down the tables after lunch, Todd picked up a balled napkin and threw it at me. I caught it midair and tossed it back. "Maybe we should play a game of ping pong instead," Todd said. "I have the next twenty minutes free."

"Good idea," I said, "especially since the director just stepped in."

We kept tossing the napkin back and forth as we walked to the activity center, so it was an easy transition to ping pong. We played two games. Each of us tried to outdo the other by putting a spin on the ball and hitting outside the other's reach. We laughed each time the ball spiked off the corner of the table. I won one; Todd won the other.

When we gave each other the high-five, I let him squeeze my hand. "See you later tonight," he said. "You're coming to the counselors' party here in the center, aren't you?"

I nodded. "I'm planning on it. See you then."

After all the kids were asleep, the party finally started. When I arrived a half-hour late, Todd met me at the door and handed me a beer. A cooler filled with cans of Miller draft and bottles of hard cider sat in the corner of the room. I joined him and the other counselors in demolishing the supply. That was bad enough; what happened afterwards was worse. He and I walked into the woods, supposedly to talk about organizing a scavenger hunt. We almost ended up lying in the grass behind a clump of evergreens. I was unbuttoning my blouse when I came to my senses. "I'm getting out of here, Todd. There's a NO SEX rule in place. This summer, I'm keeping my distance. I expect you to respect that."

He'd already slipped off his t-shirt. "Don't be silly, Debs. Breaking the rule didn't bother you last year. Hooking up now and again is no big deal. All the counselors do it. If tonight doesn't work for you, let's plan a follow-up."

"No way. I'm over one-night stands. Find somebody else."

His shoulders sagged. "You're a tough one. Hope you find what you're looking for out there." He put his t-shirt back on and stalked off.

I stumbled back to my room for a few hours sleep before the breakfast bell rang. I woke up both pleased that I had dealt with Todd assertively but troubled by the erotic dream I'd had about him last night.

"Hey, Debs," Todd called out as I entered the mess hall the following morning. "How ya doin', babe? Glad you're up and at'em."

I stared at him until he looked away. "I'm fine."

Instead of walking over to my assigned table with Todd, I headed to the kitchen, hoping to avoid him by helping Sarah prepare and serve the meals. "I want to get away from Todd," I said. "He comes on to me way too much. Can I eat here after everyone else is finished?"

"You, too? I thought I was the only one. He gets away with it because he's so hot and lots of fun. Too bad he's such a loser. So, yes, you can sit at this small corner table with me. Tell the director you're sitting with the kitchen staff. He can get a counselor to take your place at the kid's table."

And that's what we did. Sarah and I ate together when the campers and their counselors were finished. Bono sometimes joined us. He usually brought me my drinks from the canteen and cleaned up my dirty dishes.

One morning I was eating lunch alone. Bono sat on the folding chair across from me. "I never expected the camp nurse to be so young," he said. "Is this a mini vacation for you? You must work in a hospital or somewhere else."

"I do. I work on the pediatric medical unit at Lehigh Valley Hospital. I'm also finishing up a nurse practitioner program in pediatrics at Penn State."

"What brings you to Sunnybrook?" He shrugged. "Must bore you to tears."

"It's great for a month. Nice break from the stress of the hospital and the pressure from school. There's such a relaxed atmosphere here, and I love the kids. At camp, work and fun are mixed together."

"I teach in a special school for autistic kids. I love getting out of the classroom and needed something to do this summer. You're right about the stress. Work here does seem like fun."

"What do you do for fun in the winter?" I asked.

"Golf in the fall and spring. Play the guitar year round. How 'bout you?"

"Me? I like music too. Listening, not playing. I used to cross country ski but haven't had spare time for ages. I plan to get out more once I'm finished with school."

"Nurse Debbie, Nurse Debbie." It was Hannah, and she was crying. "I dropped a log on my foot. My big toe. Look. It's bleeding under the nail. It hurts bad."

Bono carried her to the infirmary where I found an icepack for her toe. I had a decision to make. Send her to the ER where a doctor would cut the nail with a surgical knife to drain the blood and relieve the pressure. Or I could sterilize a needle, make a hole in the nail, and drain the blood out of it here at the camp. For that, I would need both the director and the parent's permission. While Bono spoke to the camp director, I called the parents. Fifteen minutes later Hannah lay on the infirmary cot singing "I knew an Old Lady who Swallowed a Fly" with Bono. At the same time, I drained the blood from underneath her nail with a needle I'd sterilized with the flames of a fire lighter stick..

After dinner one evening, Bono and I lingered over dessert. "What are your plans after college?" He took a bite of his cherry pie.

"I graduate from Penn State in December. In January, I'll start work with a pediatrician on my hospital's medical unit."

Bono stretched his legs under the table. "I've been teaching special ed for two years now. My bad foot helps me understand some of the kids' challenges. You'll do well working with the sick kids. I can tell by the way you listen to Hannah's chatter."

"Thanks. I love kids. Some of them are so brave when they're sick. They're my heroes." I sipped my coffee.

"I know what you mean. My autistic kids struggle so hard to make sense of the world. They're all my heroes."

"Now that I know you better, I see how your name fits you in some odd way. Is it your real name or a nickname?"

"Oh. It's real, all right. My mom's Irish. She named me after *The Bono*, her favorite singer who's also a human rights activist. I hated my name when I was younger, but now I like it. In Italian, the name means *good*."

"Ah, that's kinda' neat to have a legacy to your name. I like my name, but it's so common and doesn't stand for anything special."

Just then, the camp director approached the table. He looked at me. "Debbie, will you help Todd monitor the kids training for the Special Olympics this afternoon? They're meeting at the beach in ten minutes."

"Can someone else do it?" Dammit. No way did I want to be stuck with Todd at the beach.

The director squinted at me and frowned. "Any reason? Todd's concerned someone may fall and get hurt."

I nodded. "Having a nurse there is a good idea. I best grab my first-aid bag and head down ASAP." Stay close to the kids, away from Todd. You'll be fine, I told myself.

The director handed me a stopwatch. "Good. I'll tell Todd you're headed there now."

Todd and I stood on the opposite ends of the track he'd set up to time the six boys running from one end of the field to the other. I forced myself to focus on the kids and not stare at Todd's broad shoulders and lean chest muscles. It was easier than I thought.

Brian, a Ewing sarcoma survivor who'd lost his hand and part of his forearm, was the slowest. Just as he crossed the finish line for the final run, he stumbled and fell, then rolled onto the grass and hugged his knee. "I'm hurt. I can't get up," he cried.

"I'm coming." I grabbed my first-aid bag and rushed toward him. Todd stood a few feet away joking with the other kids. So like him to stay away from the serious stuff and not ask how he could help.

Moments later I stood at Brian's side. He was sitting up. "I'm scared," he cried. Blood dripped from the jagged two-inch gash on his knee and pooled on the grass under him.

Tears ran down his cheeks. "I'll never be able to run the race," he sobbed. "Hannah will kill me. She and I are partners in the two-man relay."

I pulled off my sweatshirt and applied pressure to the wound to staunch the bleeding. Once the bleeding stopped, I cleaned the wound with hydrogen peroxide. "See. It's not as bad as it looks," I said as he tentatively gazed down at his leg while I bandaged his knee. "You'll need a few stitches though." I gave him my hand to help him stand up.

"No, I won't go to the hospital. They'll examine me and find something wrong with my leg beside the cut, like the doctor did when the pain in my arm turned out to be cancer. The chemo and the surgery were awful." He swung his affected arm back and forth.

I rubbed his shoulder. "No, Brian. Your knee only needs a few stitches, nothing more. In fact this is simple enough to be handled in an urgent care clinic. No hospital."

He sighed. "Okay. I've had stitches before. I guess it's not such a big deal. I get scared that when something bad happens, the cancer is coming back."

"I can understand that. You've gone through a lot of scary stuff. A few stitches and you'll be back here, good as new."

Todd walked over to join us. "How's the knee, dude? Looks as if Nurse Debs got it all fixed up." When he pinched my butt behind Brian's back, I slapped his hand. Such an asshole. How could I ever have found him attractive?

A tear ran down Brian's cheek. "No, I need stitches."

"No problem. How 'bout Uncle Todd here drives you in his pick-up?"

"Can we blast your stereo?"

"Yeah, man, we will blast the stereo, and you get to pick the music. Since we'll miss lunch, we'll have to stop at Burger King. If we're still hungry, Dairy Queen is across the street."

After Brian and Todd left, I watched the rest of the kids kick a soccer ball around. No one wanted to race any more. Soon it was noon. The kids headed up to their cabins to wash up for lunch. Even though it was early, I walked directly to the mess hall, hoping I'd have some time to talk with Bono.

Typical Bono. He was busy working in the kitchen when I sat down on a stool away from his work area.

He stopped slicing apples and walked over to sit on a stool beside me. "What's up?" he asked. "You look beat."

"I am. You'll never believe my morning." I sighed, then, told him my story.

"I'm so sorry." He ran his hand through his shoulder length hair. "That kid's been through a lot." He handed me a Granny Smith apple.

I took a bite. "I know. He was scared to death to go to the hospital, so many bad memories there."

He grabbed another apple and bit into it. "We need to do something special to surprise him. I'll bake cupcakes, chocolate ones like my mom used to make for my birthdays."

"Awesome idea," I said. "Once dinner's over, let's take the gang down to the lake to eat their cupcakes there. It will still be daylight, and we can play some circle games, like *Animal Alphabet*. Make it more special."

"Good idea." He squeezed my hand.

"I'll fill a garbage bag with blankets and take it to the beach now. We all need to sit on blankets. I saw lots of bugs down there yesterday."

"See you later then." Bono left to help the kitchen staff finish dinner preparations and bake the cupcakes while I headed to the lake.

Hannah and two of her friends, Ashley and Brianna, rushed up to me as I was coming back from the lake. I'd just placed the blankets on a grassy area where we all could sit. "Nurse Debbie, Brianna got bad bites on her legs," Hannah exclaimed.

Mosquitoes were the likely culprits, but on closer inspection, I realized they were tick bites. Removing the ticks would be tricky but leaving the pincers embedded in the skin could result in Lyme disease. "Come to the infirmary," I told the girls. "There are tiny bugs in those bites. I need to get my special tweezers to remove them."

Tears filled Brianna's eyes. "Bugs inside my legs?" She began sobbing.

"Not inside your body. Just on your skin, but I'm going to get them out."

After wiping the areas with alcohol, I was able to grab the tick's head and gently coax the entire tick out with my pointed tip tweezers. Since Briana begged me to let her friends stay with her, I agreed that Ashley and Hannah could watch.

"Now we know what to do if we get bit," Ashley said.

Minutes later, a pick-up truck pulled into the camp. "It's Brian and Todd," Hannah yelled as she ran out to meet them. Todd lifted Brian out of the truck. Brian's knee had been neatly bandaged, and he walked into the mess hall with a slight limp. I hugged him. "How did it go?" I asked.

"I did good in the clinic, Nurse Debbie. Once I got there, I wasn't so scared. It was different from the hospital."

He looked at Hannah. "I won't be able to do the relay with you tomorrow," he said.

"I didn't want to do it anyway." She bent down and kissed the bandage on his leg.

"You're a brave boy, Brian," I said. "Look at you. Your knee is all fixed." I hugged him.

Lois Gerber: Second Chances

"I have to go back next week to get the stitches out. Todd will take me again. He's cool. He bought me a burger and an Oreo Blizzard at Dairy Queen."

"Wow, that's a huge treat." I had to give Todd credit; he did know how to keep the kids entertained. "Did getting the stitches hurt?"

Brian looked at his knee. "Not much. I felt brave, thinking of Bono and his leg. It'd been hurt same as mine. Now I'm like Bono." He smiled.

"Indeed you are," I said.

He turned toward the mess hall. "I want to show him my bandage."

Hannah tugged at my blouse. "Will his leg be okay? she asked. "He won't have to get it cut off, will he, like his arm?"

"No, Sweetheart. In a couple of weeks, he'll be as good as new."

"I love Brian. I wanted to be in that race with him, but now I think it's stupid."

***

"We have a surprise tonight," the camp director told the kids once they'd finished dinner. "Cupcakes outside. Bono made them special for all of you but especially for Brian, who as you all know, needed to have stitches in his leg today."

Several boys yelled, "Yeah, Brian," We all went outside to a grassy play area. I handed each kid a blanket from the pile I'd made earlier. Everyone wanted to sit next to Brian, so Bono and I put him in the center of a circle with the other kids in the periphery.

Bono passed out the cupcakes, ones he'd iced in yellow frosting and decorated with happy faces. Several girls sang, "We love Bono; he's our hero."

Bono lifted Brian on his back and carried him around the circle. Soon he was giving all the kids piggyback rides as I

44

cleaned up the mess from the cupcakes. Meanwhile, the girls changed their chant to "We love Brian; he's our man."

After we played a few circle games, the kids broke up in small groups to sit and talk. Hannah and Andrew, a thirteen-year-old who'd been cognitively impaired after his recovery from meningitis, walked over to sit on the clump of grass next to Bono and me.

"Hannah and Andrew hang out together a lot. They sure seem to like each other," Bono said.

I gazed at them. "So far it's a friendship. Not sure what will happen next year. Hannah is so loving. I don't think there's anyone she doesn't care about."

The two appeared very content as they looked in each other's eyes and giggled softly. Andrew was picking clover leaves and making a bouquet of them. Hannah's brown hair fluttered in the gentle breeze. When he handed her the clovers, she kissed him on the cheek. I had a fleeting wish that I was so innocent.

Bono looked at them too. "I remember bringing a bouquet of dandelions to the girl who lived next door. I was six years old. She kissed me on the cheek just like Hannah kissed Andrew. For days, I didn't want to wash my face."

"Yes, and then we grow up."

"Any guys you wish would kiss you on the cheek?"

"I've had a couple relationships. Last one ended a few weeks ago. Alec didn't want to commit."

"That stinks."

"Maybe I don't have this boy/girl thing down right. Now I want to just have a relationship with myself."

"My girlfriend broke up with me in February. Said I was too much of a risk taker. She was right, but I wanted her to give me another chance. My limp's from a motorcycle accident on the Pocono Raceway. She left me soon after the smash-up. I don't ride anymore."

"Bummer."

"I was furious she left the way she did." He blinked and looked away.

"I understand." I hadn't planned to tell Bono about Todd, but somehow it felt right to tell him what had happened between Todd and me.

Bono raised his eyebrows. "Thanks for sharing that. I'd already heard the story from Sarah, but I like that you trust me enough to explain."

"It wasn't easy. I realized how stupid I was to get involved with him last summer. I guess hindsight has its benefits. Took me a while to see the light though."

The kids were running wild. I looked at my watch. "Time to get the hellions back to the cabins."

Bono stood and held out his hand to help me up. "Let's get on it."

***

After dinner one evening I sat in my bedroom getting caught up on my emails. Caitlyn and Marsha, two counselors in the girls' units, knocked on my door. I invited them in. We sat around the kitchen table, each of us nursing a glass of diet Coke.

"We want your advice on our girls and their budding hormones," Marsha said. "All the kids talk about is sex, hair styles, or their boobs."

Caitlyn interrupted her. "My twelve-year-olds found my bras and were trying them on over their clothes. It was kinda' funny, but I had to reprimand them and make them give them back."

"They all think they are too fat," Marsha said. "Only a couple of them are chubby. Most are just fine."

46

"The way they fix each other's hair and overdo make-up. It's cute."

The counselors cared about the kids, and most of the children sensed it. Marsha leaned forward. "Yesterday, Ashley told me how she liked you, Debbie, that you listened but didn't tell her what to do like her mom and dad."

"Ashley and Brianna approached me yesterday," Caitlyn said. "They're concerned about their cabin buddy, Lisa. They said she snuck out of their cabin several nights ago to make out with Derek, one of the boy campers."

"Let me think more about this," I said. "Then maybe I can bring Lisa in to talk. Her hormones have definitely kicked in. She's quite physically mature for a thirteen-year-old."

This conversation would be tricky. After all I'd done some pretty wild things, even here at camp and I didn't want to project the image of an uptight adult or nurse who acted judgmental and out of touch. Yet this was an opportunity to help Lisa deal appropriately with her sexuality. The book, *Girling Up*, covered topics like this. The next day I drove to town and picked up a copy.

The following afternoon, Caitlyn brought Lisa over to my living area in the infirmary, where we could sit at my kitchen table to talk. Bono had made peanut butter cookies and strawberry milk shakes for us. After a few minutes small talk, Caitlyn said, "Nurse Debbie wants to talk to you about sneaking out of the cabin the other night. I'm leaving so the two of you can talk privately."

I said good-bye to Caitlyn and turned toward Lisa. "What happened the other night with you and Derek?" I asked.

Lisa slurped her milk shake, "I didn't do anything wrong."

I glanced at the *Girling Up* book that I'd set on the table. "Yeah, but sneaking out after curfew is against the rules."

"Derek and I were just talking. I'm not a slut just because Derek and I kissed a couple of times." Tears filled her eyes.

"I never said you were a slut."

"What do you care if Derek and I make out?"

I looked at her green-dyed hair and heavy make-up. "Because I care about you and your future and don't want to see you sexually involved before you're ready." I took a deep breath.

"Derek makes me feel good. So what if we do more?"

"At thirteen, you're not ready for more. First you need to understand who you are and what you really want in a boyfriend." I held up the book. "This book looks at life from a teen's perspective. You're welcome to borrow it."

"No thanks. You sound just like my mother. I'm outta here." She grabbed a cookie and left.

I headed to my bedroom. What should I have said differently? Did I really sound like an old stodgy and out of touch? Maybe what I told Lisa is what I would tell my daughter and what I wish my mother had told me. Yet our conversation went wrong somewhere. I had so much more to learn about teen age sexuality.

Later that day, Bono and I sat on a beach towel watching the kids play in the shallow lake water. I sifted my fingers through the sand. Bono moved his towel close to mine. "The kids really like you," he said.

"Some of them, maybe." I told him my conversation with Lisa. "Not sure about her."

Bono rubbed his chin. "It's funny how they can frustrate the hell out of you but are so sweet at the same time. They really look up to us even when they act disrespectful."

I brushed a mosquito from his shoulder and let my hand linger for a moment. "Sometimes we're almost more important than their peers and, for sure, their parents. What you told her probably sunk in more than you think."

"Nurse Debbie, Nurse Debbie, Andrew's drowning!"

How things could change in a second. Hannah stood waist deep in water. She pointed to Andrew in the center of the lake. He was dogpaddling to keep his head above water. Bono grabbed the lifesaving float sitting on the beach and threw it toward him. Andrew didn't seem to understand what to do, and we rushed into the water, clothes and all. I prayed understood his situation and would not panic.

He didn't. By the time we got there, Andrew stood chest high in the water. He brushed seaweed from his face and smoothed down his curly blond hair. "I'm okay. I swam in over my head by mistake. Never went under," he said with a silly grin on his face. "I want to stay and play in the water." He splashed Hannah on the back.

The other kids circled around Andrew clapping.

I took a deep breath as Bono and I brought in the float. Bono had taken off his t-shirt. A two-inch scar ran across his shoulder.

"The motorcycle accident?" I asked.

He nodded.

I ran my fingers over the raised area. "My cousin had a Suzuki. He got hurt too. I'm glad you don't ride anymore."

He took my hand and brushed it to his lips. My body tingled with excitement.

Bono and I watched the campers play a few games of *Marco Polo* with the kids, then once the kids had dried off, I paired the boys and girls up and Bono marched them back to camp for lemonade and cookies.

***

The last night in camp, the counselors planned a bonfire on the beach by the lake. The fire was aglow, thanks to the guys who had the embers burning when Bono and I brought the children to the beach. We showed the kids how to make s'mores and listened to their ghost stories. Todd showed up with a few drums and maracas. Before long everyone had an instrument, even me.

Bono played the guitar and made up silly ditties like, "I really think you're sweet and oh so very neat with boots upon your feet."

The kids laughed and clapped. "More" they begged. After that we all sang some traditional campfire songs. "She'll be Coming Round the Mountain," and "Kumbaya," the song Harry Belafonte made popular, were ones I remembered from my childhood.

Later, Bono came over and took my hand. "Can I call you when we get home?"

Feeling tongue-tied and not sure what to say, I nodded.

He smiled. "I don't bite. Here's my e-mail address and cell phone number. You call me."

"Okay." I put the slip of paper in my pocket. He squeezed my hand. His fingers were strong yet sensitive.

My heart pounded. "I like you a lot, but I wasn't planning to have a camp romance this year. I can't even tell you when I'll be ready. Another thing is that your name and how it stands for goodness, is perfect for you."

He drew me to him in a quick embrace. "If and whenever you're ready. I sense
something special between us."

The kids circled us. "Bono loves Nurse Debbie," they chanted.

We both laughed. "Looks as if it's time to break up the campfire, get you all settled in before you all head home tomorrow. "

"You little ruffians, get movin'," he told the kids.

I looked at Bono. "See you in the morning."

Right before the lights went out that night, Hannah cornered me in the bathroom. "What's love, Nurse Debbie? Is it when you feel close to a boy? Like when I knew Andrew needed me when he tripped in the water?"

I swallowed hard. "That's part of love, Hannah."

"Or is it when you talk back and forth about silly stuff? Andrew and I talk about how we blow bubbles in our milk with our straws, make banana and peanut butter sandwiches, and why dogs always lick their noses. He listens to me and smiles a lot."

"Listening's real important, Hannah."

"He makes me feel happy and gooey on the inside. He's my heart's sun now."

I put my arms around her. "You have it in a nutshell. Part of love is feeling good when you're around someone and talking to them about everyday things. Another part is that gooey feeling."

Here I thought I was Hannah's mentor. Tonight it was the other way around. I thought about Bono. I needed to make a decision.

Bono listens to me. He makes me laugh. He makes me feel safe. I can tell him what I'm thinking. What am I waiting for? I've found my sun.

I reached into my pocket for my I-phone to punch in Bono's e-mail address and cell number. I'd need that information if I missed him tomorrow morning.

Starting Over

Sirens shattered the midnight darkness outside the hospital window. Minutes later the riveting words, **Code Blue**, echoed from the intercom. I left the nurses station in the surgical step-down unit and rushed to the emergency room to join the team treating a thirty-two-year-old man bleeding from a gunshot wound to the abdomen.

I clamped two blood vessels with sterile forceps. A resident cauterized several more. All the while another nurse was applying intermittent pressure to the patient's wound. As soon his bleeding stopped and his vital signs were stable, he was rushed to the operating room for the surgeon to repair the gut trauma he'd sustained.

My nursing supervisor stopped me as I left the ER. "The patient's that young priest who runs the inner-city parish on Fulton Road. He's the one who organized the food program and vocational training for the poor. He works with kids, trying to bring racial harmony to the city. A homeless man he's been trying to help get off drugs shot him."

"I've read articles about him online and in the *Cleveland Plain Dealer*."

She nodded. "You kept your cool in there. Good job."

***

Several days later Father Timothy was transferred to the surgical step-down area, a small unit with twelve private rooms. He was a handsome man, not much older than me, with an athletic physique and well-trimmed wavy blond hair. I was assigned to give him care and was drawn to his eyes, a bright steel gray, such a contrast to his somber expression and the stubble on his face. For a moment, I thought of Father Paul, the priest of my childhood parish but immediately sensed Father Timothy was different somehow and not so twisted.

The next evening as I adjusted the flow of his IV, he looked directly at me. "Why?" he asked. "Why did Derek shoot me? He was only months away from his high school graduation. We spent hours talking about his problems with his alcoholic parents. I would have given him the money. He didn't have to shoot me for it."

I assumed he wanted a religious answer. "Maybe God is testing you, preparing you for something bigger."

"Maybe." He groaned as he pulled himself up in his bed. "Can I call you Kathleen?' he asked. "Or do you prefer Ms. Preston? "Your nametag reads Kathleen Preston RN, so I'm not sure. One of the nurse's aides told me you're not married."

"Call me Kathleen, and she's right. I'm not married, never have been." I ran my fingers down my pink scrubs.

"Ah Kathleen, I used to think heartbreaking trauma like my gunshot wound happened for a higher reason. Now I'm not so sure." His whole body trembled, and I took his hand.

I sensed his spiritual despair, perhaps similar to my own. That's why I worked the night shift, so I could sleep in the daylight where the memory of Father Paul's body against mine faded.

"There is so much about life we don't understand." I squeezed his hand. "Would you like me to have the chaplain see you?"

"He's already been here. A nice man, but this is something I must work out by myself."

I'd always been an independent person, so I understood that desire; yet my mind searched for an appropriate answer. "I'd like to hear what you're thinking. Let me know if you change your mind about the chaplain. Getting over an assault like yours takes time." My response sounded shallow, even to me.

He sighed and said, "Thank you. I appreciate that."

One night, Father Timothy woke up in a panic, gasping for air. His eyes, wide opened, were riveted to the window with fear. His arms thrashed against the sides of his mattress. I alerted staff and rushed to him. "Don't kill me," he screamed. I held his hands until his shaking stopped.

"A panic attack," the hospitalist said. "He's quiet now. I've ordered Ativan in case it happens again."

"I'm so sorry," Father Timothy said. "Did I scare you?'

"A little, but it's all right. I understand."

After that, I spent as much time at his bedside as I could. When his fingers brushed mine, my throat tightened. Electricity shot through my body. Hazy images of Father Paul filled my mind, images of the priest pressing himself against me, his hands covering my breasts, the swishing sound of his long black robe moving back and forth across the floor, the man who started to abuse me when I was fourteen years old.

Father Timothy told me about his inner-city congregation and their need for social service help. How he'd spent weeks counseling Derek, a nineteen-year-old parishioner addicted to meth. Our conversations seemed to calm him.

After changing his dressing one night, I ran my fingers through Father Timothy's blond curls. "Bedhead," I said. "Comb your hair." I couldn't believe what I was doing. It was against my professions standards to act out feelings of physical attraction to a patient. I quickly pulled my hand away.

He laughed. "Do it again. I feel some tangles that you missed."

"No, it's wasn't right for me to touch you like that. I'm sorry, Father."

He smiled. "Forget it."

We talked more about the shooting and how drugs made people violent and even willing to kill loved ones to support their habit. He buttoned his pajama top. "Yes, Derek has a sickness I couldn't cure. I know that now, just didn't know how bad it could get. I'm glad he's in jail. Only hope he gets the help he needs."

"Would you have done anything different if you had a chance to relive that night?"

"I shouldn't have let him in my office unless there was someone with me, and giving him money also was wrong. We discussed rehab and counseling from the start, but a psychologist would have said I enabled him and he would have been right."

"A lesson learned then?"

"A lesson learned too late. Yet I'm sure God had his reasons to let this happen."

Two days later he was out of bed and scheduled to be transferred to the general surgical floor.

Before the aide came to move him, Father Timothy said, "You've been a wonderful nurse, Kathleen, the one who's helped me sort out my confusion and anger even more than the priests who visit. I'll miss you."

"I'll miss you too." I swallowed hard. "I'll stop in sometime and check on you in your new room." Tears filled my eyes as he was wheeled down the hall.

***

Three days after his transfer, I sat on a chair beside Father's bed. His hands lay on his bedside tray. After a few minutes of chit chat, he said, "I've done a lot of thinking while I've been in the hospital, Kathleen. I'm almost well enough to go back to work, but I want to do something different. I plan to ask Monsignor Anthony to back a project to provide comprehensive services to the homeless in our city; some place the poor can stay, get basic health care, food and shelter, even job training. Would you help me? I need a health professional like you to bounce ideas off of." He cocked his head to the side as if waiting for a 'yes' answer.

I gasped, realizing our relationship wouldn't have to end here. It took my breath away at how events that seemed bad at the time could end in a good way. "Yes, I'd love to, Father. I can come on my days off and perhaps some evenings before work."

"Call me Tim, Kathleen. We'll be working together. I want to get the grant for the homeless project written soon."

"You've really thought this out. What's the timeline?"

"I'm not sure yet. Come over to the rectory in a couple of weeks and we can talk about the important points to include in the grant and develop an outline to give to the monsignor. I should feel stronger by then."

We scheduled a time and date.

***

As I walked up the winding brown cobblestone driveway to the rectory grounds, I was overcome by the beautiful and peaceful surroundings. The hundred-year-old red brick building and several smaller units were set between acres of pine trees and several small ponds. Chirping birds reminded me of the deep connection between nature and man. I took a deep breath. The tension that I'd been feeling lately in my shoulder muscles vanished.

We met in the foyer. "Come into the conference room," he suggested. "We can work in there."

I sat down at the worn oak table directly across from him. A stack of papers and several pens lay on the table. Plain white cotton curtains covered the windows. A crucifix and a large portrait of Pope Francis hung above the mantle. An old upright piano stood against one wall next to a beige upholstered sofa.

"It's so good to see you," he said.

I laughed to cover up my feeling of insecurity. "It's good to see you too."

He smiled. "You seem nervous, different than you were in the hospital."

"Fath…, I mean Tim, I am nervous. And I feel funny with just the two of us here together. It's strange seeing you outside the hospital and wearing your clerical collar."

He gave me a slow lopsided grin. "I'm still the same person. Just a little stronger. Let's talk a bit before we start working."

I tapped my fingers on the table. "I don't know what to say to you, what to talk about besides your injury and what I can do to help you heal."

"Start by telling me about yourself, your family, what you like, what is the most important thing in the world to you? You never speak about yourself."

"In nursing schools we're taught not to talk about ourselves, so I'm more a listener than a talker."

"How do you spend your days off?"

I shrugged. "I work out at the gym a couple days a week, play my electric keyboard, and do a bit of cooking. I love to cook and try out new recipes. Saturday evenings my single friends and I follow several bands who play in the local restaurants and bars."

"Do you have a boyfriend?"

I picked a thread from a loose button and watch it drift to the ground. "Kind of. This guy, Dan, and I have dated for a few months. He's a pharmacist at the CVS in town."

Tears filled my eyes. Suddenly I was fourteen again and working in Father Paul's office. At first I emptied his wastebaskets and washed out his coffee maker. Then, he asked me to fold the Sunday bulletins and sort his mail. I loved sitting at his mahogany desk by a white marble statue of the Virgin Mary while I worked.

One day, as I was ready to leave, he embraced me in a tight hug that lasted uncomfortably long. I could feel his heartbeat through my blouse. Waves of excitement burst through my body.

Afterwards, he pulled back and placed his hands on my shoulders. "Look at me, Kathleen," he said.

I forced myself to meet his gaze. I felt my face redden.

His brown eyes bore through me. "You are a special girl and so beautiful. Promise me you won't tell anyone about our hugs. They would never understand."

I whispered, "I promise."

We hugged goodbye like this, always with our clothes on, for weeks. Each time I never wanted the moments to end.

I'll never forget the afternoon he said he was moving to Boston, that he'd always care about me, that I must never tell anyone about our relationship and to remember that we never had our clothes off. I begged him to stay. When I told him how much I loved him, he pushed me away. Now after all these years, these mixed feelings of desire and guilt had resurfaced.

Tim's deep-set eyes looked at me with gentleness. "Kathleen, I don't understand what's making you sad."

"You remind me of Father Paul." I blinked back tears.

"And who is this Father Paul?"

"A priest I knew as a kid and felt connected to. For months I talked to a therapist about him. She helped me put some things about him in perspective, but then it got too hard and I quit going. I thought I was over the guilt and anger, but I guess I'm not."

"Something serious happened. You've been hurt." He laid his hand over mine.

I told him my story. "It was my fault. I made him touch me. I wanted him." Tim was a patient listener, asking just the right questions, even better than my therapist, and murmuring just the right responses.

Tim sighed. "Your Father Paul was sick, mentally sick. He was wrong and should be reported to the bishop, then the cardinal. He violated you. You were a child. He was an adult, a priest, a person you should have been able to trust. You aren't bad. You aren't damaged goods. It wasn't your fault. You are a beautiful woman with a lot to give to the world and to a man if you choose. I'm so sorry it Father Paul treated you that way."

"A year after he moved to Boston, I read in the paper that he died in an auto accident, and I felt relieved that he couldn't hurt me or any other girls anymore."

"And, at that time, you never told your parents what was going on?"

"No. My mother became very religious after my dad died. He had a heart attack when I was twelve."

"Such a lot to carry by yourself." He squeezed my hand.

Each week I shared more of my past with Tim. How after Father Paul moved away, I stopped going to church and wanted nothing to do with religion. How I spent my weekends with a group of high school friends who partied, drank beer, and smoked weed. How I dated guys until they wanted to get serious, then broke it off without explanation. My foot tapped up and down on the floor as I talked. "I really liked this guy, Alex, and we almost had sex in the backseat of his car, but in the end, all these images of Father Paul floated through my head, and I couldn't do it. Until today I wasn't sure I could be any guy's girlfriend."

"Until today?"

"For years, every once in a while I would dream I'm lying in Father Paul's arms and wake up screaming for him to get off me. Last night, my dream was different. Last night I dreamt I was a priest and he the parishioner. He asked me for forgiveness, and we both cried as if to say we were sorry." My voice shook as I spoke.

"An impactful dream, Kathleen. Do you think that means you've forgiven him?"

"I hope so. I don't blame myself so much anymore, and it's all because of the dream and talking with you." I stared at the clock on the wall to keep myself from leaning over and kissing his cheek.

"That's a huge step, Kathleen. We're helping each other," he said.

I nodded and wiped the tears from my face.

"So many losses you've had. You'd never know it from the way you nursed me in the hospital and how you healed me from the inside out."

"Sometimes I think nursing is in my blood."

"In some ways you and I are a lot alike. We're both only children. My dad died when I was in junior high. I was a maverick kid, had lots of friends but no focus. Hardly made it through high school. Decided at nineteen to enter the seminary. Realized then that the priesthood was in my blood. I fought the urge for a while since my mom begged me to marry and have children."

"Really?"

"Part of me thought the priesthood was for sissies, but I could never find a job that I liked. I had girlfriends through my early twenties but am celibate now. Never fit deeply in any woman's life."

He took a deep breath. "Even after I was ordained and the bishop assigned me to a suburban church, I was confused about my role. I didn't feel I was reaching the parishioners or making any difference in their lives. And then Derek shot me.

60

Forgiveness. I never suspected it would be so complicated." He picked up his pen and squeezed it.

"Forgiveness and understanding others is horribly difficult. The summer after I graduated from high school, I was moping around the house and crying a lot. My mom made me see a therapist. I started to tell her about the abuse but never said it was a priest who violated me. It was too hard to talk about and I stopped going. I owe her though. She helped me enroll in the community college and insisted I find something comforting to do while I decided what to do with my life. Lucky I found meaning and even comfort in nursing and socializing with my friends."

He took a deep breath. "Aside from prayer and helping the parishioners, my only comforts were riding my motorcycle and playing the piano. I always liked classical music."

"Tim, I can't believe this. I play the piano too. Love classical music, especially Beethoven." A fluttery feeling spread through my belly.

"I heard that from the other nurses in the hospital. Does your music comfort you now?"

"Yes, playing my keyboard soothes me. But keep going. I want to hear more about you."

"After two years, the diocese transferred me here to St. Rocco's, an older church in a poor neighborhood. The new parish saved me, gave me a purpose. The inner-city people became my life."

"I've heard so much about the changes you've brought to the neighborhoods."

"I've done my best, maybe not enough."

"What do you mean?" I reached out to squeeze his arm.

He pulled back. "I still don't understand all the reasons why Derek shot me, why God would let that happen."

"I can see how the shooting challenged your faith, just like Father Paul's abusing me challenged mine."

"It was hard to accept. I felt mixed up for a long time."

He bit his lip. "I think I'm back and doing what I should be with my life. I was called to this work. I don't like much of the church ritual, but the priesthood fulfills me, gives me the opportunity to get inside people's heads, make social changes, connect people to God and nature."

"Sounds as if your doubts made it stronger."

He sighed. "They have. I've never told anyone, not even the monsignor, all this about my past before."

"You're lucky you didn't have a Father Paul in your life," I said. "You look like him but are so different."

He smiled. "Enough talking. We need to get down to business."

As we sat across from each other working on the grant, my body stirred as my physical attraction to Tim grew. One afternoon he rubbed his hand across my cheek. I wanted to rub my finger over his lips but instead pulled the car keys out of my pocket and forced myself to leave.

One evening months later, he said, "Play the piano with me, Kathleen. My favorite piece is Beethoven's *Moonlight Sonata*. Do you know it?"

"A favorite of mine too."

We sat side by side on the scratched up piano bench with a wobbly leg. Our hands moved in unison as our fingers hit the keys. The sound of the music filled my chest. I felt at one with the world, with Tim. I looked into his eyes and let my lips brush his cheek. "Will you hug me?" I asked.

He pulled away and took a deep breath. "My vows. I can't break them. I can't hurt you like Father Paul did." His squeezed his eyes shut. When he opened them, tears ran down his cheeks.

"It's my choice this time, Tim. I'm not fourteen anymore, and you're not like Father Paul."

"I'm the one who bears the responsibility for our relationship." He shook his head. What you're suggesting isn't right."

"Love is never wrong," I said.

He trembled as he nodded and lifted the silver cross from his neck and placed it on the table.

He took me in his arms, and we swayed softly. The *Moonlight Sonata* was still playing in my head. An image of Father Paul filled my head for a moment, and I almost pulled away from Tim, but I squeezed my eyes shut and forced myself to make the image fade.

I opened my eyes and looked up at Tim. Our faces touched. The heat of his breath caressed my cheek. My body relaxed and the world fell away.

His hand was soft and gentle as he led me to the sofa.

"I want you so much, but I'm nervous," I whispered.

"Tell me if it feels wrong and I'll stop."

I shook my head. "I'm scared because it feels right."

Afterwards, we lay intertwined in each other's arms. I looked up into his steel gray eyes. A single tear dropped onto my cheek. I didn't brush it away. I wanted it to dry there forever.

The next day, I felt radiant, different somehow. Tim, oh Tim! You changed my life, opened up a whole new world for me. Tears welled up in my eyes as I realized my relationship with him couldn't last. It was wrong for both of us, yet I couldn't break away.

Months passed. Tim and I finished writing the grant. Now we met only occasionally to make love. Growing more uncomfortable visiting the rectory under false pretenses, I suggested we meet at my favorite restaurant to talk.

We sat at a table close to the piano where a young girl played Chopin's *Fantaisie Impromptu.* "I can't keep coming to the rectory now that the grant has been submitted." I took a bite of my prime rib.

He sipped his wine. "I know but I have news. The diocese has approved our grant to run the shelter as part of an inner-city church's training program. The problem is that the church is in Chicago, not Cleveland."

I gasped. "That's three hundred miles away."

"Not that far," he said.

"Oh my God. I had no idea this would happen. You never told me that was a possibility. When did you find out?" My throat closed around my words.

He wiped a smudge of spaghetti sauce from his lip. "Yesterday. I told Father Anthony I wasn't sure I wanted to move to Chicago. He was upset and implied I needed to follow his directive. You could come along to help me start up the program once it's established. We'd have to live apart and keep our visits secret though."

"Are you serious?" I was so upset, I pointed my fork at him as I spoke.

"Yes," he said. "Then, once the program is running smoothly, I could leave the priesthood, and we could get married, perhaps in a couple years. In the meantime I could go back to school to earn a social work degree. I'd have to take online classes at night. We can travel back and forth and see each other a few days a month. It wouldn't be that different from what we're doing now."

I took a deep breath and glared at him. "You have to be kidding. A five or six hour commute for a day or two a month for a couple of years. That's a lot to ask and it's crazy. You could leave the church and find a job and go to school here."

"The work there is something I need to do. You could move to Chicago with me."

"Quit Memorial Hospital? Start all over? I won't do that." I leaned forward. "My life is here in Cleveland at least for now. I'm not ready to move or to get married. To be honest, that's too many changes at one time. Plus, we could never live together if you stayed in the priesthood."

He reached across the table and took my hand. "I understand, but there is a lot going on in the Windy City. I want to be with you. We could have a good life there and see each other occasionally."

"You can't spring all this on me and sit there as if we're deciding which movie to see on a Saturday night. It's too much to think about. And here I planned to talk to you tonight about how we were going to continue seeing each other now that we no longer had the grant writing pretext, and you come up with this."

"I've come up with a solution for us."

"No, it's not our solution. It's your solution. I'm too upset to talk anymore. I'm going home. Now." I grabbed my purse and headed to the parking garage.

***

For several nights, I lay awake thinking about our conversation. I loved Tim, but I'd walled part of myself off for so long that I needed time away from him to gain a different perspective on my life. Our relationship helped me understand myself. I loved the way his body, so trim yet muscular, felt against mine. Not to mention the dimple in his chin and his quirky laugh. He was kind and attentive, a father figure and boyfriend combined. My therapist once said we set up situations in our present lives to heal problems of the past. Tim helped me heal from my childhood abuse but took advantage of me in a different way than Father Paul. First, I felt anger, then resignation, and finally determination to break off the relationship.

The following week we met at Starbucks and sat at a small corner table. I arrived a few minutes early to give myself time to compose myself. He flashed me a confident smile as he entered. We both ordered coffee and a bagel with cream cheese.

Tim ran his fingers through his hair before sitting down. "This is so hard Kathleen. I don't want to lose you but I still want to stay in the priesthood until the project is completed. Running a homeless shelter and work training program with a spiritual focus is my dream. I love you. I'm asking you again to come with me."

I shook my head as I bit into my bagel. "No. I won't go. I'm done sneaking around."

"You don't love me enough," he said.

"That's not it. I love you very much, but I won't sacrifice two years of my life for your dream. We don't have a normal relationship—no mutual friends and never doing things like going to Cedar Point, dancing in clubs, or picnicking on a Lake Erie beach. It would be the same narrow life in Chicago. You're obviously thinking of yourself, not me." I leaned forward. "Why can't you see that?" My voice sounded shrill.

"I am thinking of you, of us. I'm inviting you to come with me. Your work and our relationship always seemed enough for you." A vein in the side of his neck throbbed.

"Your words make the idea sound simple but it's time to end our relationship. I need to move on." My stomach roiled.

He bit his lip. "Perhaps you're right, Kathleen. God planned for our coming together. We gave each other hope and comfort, but you've changed. Maybe you're right that we should be apart, at least for a while. And, even though I've thought about it, I may never leave the priesthood. It's who I am."

"I don't understand. Your words almost sound rehearsed."

"Don't say that. I've prayed a lot about this. Can we at least be friends?"

I nodded. "You'll always be in my heart. You gave me back my life, the core of who I am, but I paid a heavy price." Tears ran down my cheeks as we hugged good-bye.

We left with our half-eaten bagels sitting on the plates.

I took the next day off work. I knew I'd made the right decision, but I found myself lying in bed holding a pillow and pretending it was Tim. I felt as if someone had shot me through the heart. For days I struggled to make it through my work shifts, performing my tasks by rote, treating patients in a perfunctory way.

One day Naomi, a co-worker, stopped me in the supply room. "Kathleen, something's wrong. For weeks you acted happy. All of a sudden, you're barely communicative and have pushed us all away. What's going on?"

I put my hands across my face and swayed back and forth. "I've made a decision I could regret forever."

She hugged me. "It can't be that bad, girlfriend."

"Maybe, maybe not. Remember that priest who was shot and in our ICU?"

"Of course. All of us remember him. The good looking one. And...."

"I've been helping him write a grant, and things got out of control."

Her eyes opened wide. "You've been sleeping with him. I can tell."

I started to cry and nodded half-heartedly.

"Son of a bitch. He's a priest. He should be shot. He's taking advantage of you."

"Not anymore. He's moving away. We broke up. Actually I broke it off with him. Give me some credit for that."

"He needs to be reported, and I'm not even religious."

I shook my head. "It was consensual, and I even started it. It's over. I learned a lot. It's just going to take time to readjust. Please don't tell anyone, for his sake and for mine. He left town and took his secret with him. It needs to stay that way."

She shook her head. "I won't say anything. You have my word. But I don't understand you. You're so mixed up when it comes to men."

"Not as much as I was. Tim's someone I'll always love in my own way. He came into my life at the right time and left at the right time. I'm going to start dating again."

"Good. You're off Saturday, right? A bunch of us are meeting at the Academy Tavern for a burger and a couple beers about seven. Trish, Jeff and Kevin from the pharmacy will be there."

"Is Dan Connors coming? He's part of the hospital's pharmacy group even though he works at CVS now."

"No. He's stuck working the evening shift. You used to date him, didn't you?"

"Yeah. Things got too complicated, so we broke up. He's a nice guy."

"You'll come with us Saturday, right?"

I nodded. "Yeah, I'll be there."

***

After that evening with Naomi and the gang, I gradually became more social and regained my equilibrium. One afternoon, Dan met me in the hospital cafeteria line. It had been over a year since he and I had dated.

I was embarrassed to think of our last date. We were lying on his sofa listening to music, his arms wrapped around me. When Dan unbuttoned my blouse, I jumped up. A sudden flash of Father Paul pressing himself against me took my breath away. I grabbed my sweater from a nearby chair. "Take me home," I demanded that evening. "Right now." Dan asked me what was wrong. "I feel a bad migraine coming on. I need to go home." I broke up with him the following day.

I'd changed a lot since that night so long ago. "It's good to see you again, Dan," I said as I studied the sandwich selections.

"Good to see you, too, Kathleen." He took a glass of iced tea from the cooler. "I've been meaning to call you. Maybe we could go to dinner and start over again, that is if you're not seeing someone else."

"Yes, I would love that." I sensed our relationship would be different this time. Thanks to Tim, I no longer thought about Father Paul when I was with a man. And Dan was cute with an athletic build and easy smile like Tim, but he was taller and his hair and eyes were dark brown.

Dan and I resumed our relationship. Soon we were spending hours together—dancing in the local clubs, watching Netflix movies, and partying aboard his pontoon boat on Lake Erie. I met his parents and brothers and sister, something I never did with Tim. We talked for hours about our childhoods. When I told him about Father Paul and Tim, he listened carefully. Our lovemaking began with hugging and kissing. Soon we spent hours in bed lying in each other's arms. Being with Dan was the most natural thing in the world.

I saw Tim on his occasional trips back to Cleveland. We met for coffee at Starbucks. He kept me up to date on the progress he'd made at St. Patrick's. I talked about my job and the enjoyable activities I'd been doing with Dan and my nursing friends. He offered his congratulations when I emailed him that Dan and I were engaged.

He did not accept the invitation to our wedding but came to Cleveland the week before. We met for coffee at Starbucks near the Hilton where he was staying.

As we sipped our lattes, I shared our plans to marry at the Holy Rosary Church and honeymoon in Barbados. Tim spoke of life in Chicago, the parishioners at his church and the symphony concerts he'd seen at the Lincoln Center.

Before he parted that afternoon, he handed me a small silver box.

"What's this?" I asked.

Tim smiled. "A wedding gift. Open it."

I lifted the lid to find a silver charm attached to a key ring. "It's beautiful," I said. "A dove, a white one." Joyful tears filled my eyes.

"A parting present," he said. "For you and Dan to start a new life. It's meant to bring you peace, love, luck and prosperity."

We hugged each other good-bye. I never heard from him again.

***

I looked back on my life as Dan and I celebrated our twenty-fifth wedding anniversary in Barbados. Those years between our honeymoon and the present have passed in a blur. Dan and our three sons are the center of my world, a place I come back to when my soul needs replenishing.

The previous year I'd accepted a promotion to be the nurse manager of Memorial's neurological ICU. I was happy with my work, organizing the unit's activities and mentoring the new nurses but saving some hours of my day for patient care.

Although we weren't active members of the local Catholic Church, Christian values were the backdrop of how we lived our lives and raised our boys. We attended mass periodically but never became active members.

I read about Tim in the newspaper. Once I even saw him celebrated on CNN as an icon of the church. That was the only way I kept up with his activities after I married. I sometimes wondered if he ever thought of me.

***

I was driving Matthew, my oldest son, back to college after spring break. He sat in the passenger seat playing a video game on his cell phone. He laid his phone on his lap and looked over at me. "I know it's my last year at Ohio State, but I want to drop out of college, quit computer science and enroll in the seminary to become a priest." His head was head cocked to the side and his face held a lopsided grin.

My hands shook so hard I nearly lost control of the car. "Why?" I stammered. "You've put so much into your studies. It would be like starting over."

He shrugged. "I guess it's my calling," he answered. "I've tried to push it away, since it seems like a hard life, especially if I can't have a girlfriend."

I pulled off the road and took the car keys out of the ignition, then took a deep breath. "Have you been thinking about this a while?" I looked into his steel gray eyes as I fingered the white dove charm in my pocket.

"Yeah. I never talked about going into the priesthood, hoping the feeling would go away, but it hasn't. I wonder where it comes from."

I sighed, remembering something my therapist once said. *Parents often have a story their children can hardly imagine.* "I'm not sure. Some people say our destiny's determined before we're born, maybe from our genes. Changing your major and entering the seminary is a big decision, a lot to think about."

"I wish I'd figured it out sooner."

I put my arms around him. "Never say that. Many of us need second chances to get our lives right. As long as you know why, starting over isn't a bad thing"

I handed Matthew the key chain. Too bad you didn't know your real father. He never knew I was pregnant with his child. "I'll let you drive from here. Once we get to Columbus, we're going to Starbucks. I have a lot I need to tell you."

My Lucky Day

My neighbor insisted I needed to see a therapist. I'd complained to her for weeks how much I wanted to be married, but that I couldn't keep a man for more than a few months. She suggested I talk to one of her friends, a nurse psychologist, Lauren Martin, who specialized in relationships. I'd always thought therapists did more harm than good, but my neighbor convinced me to give counseling a try.

I checked Lauren out on the Internet. Lots of positive reviews. She'd taught psychiatric nursing for years at the local community college until she became certified as a psychologist and then opened her private practice. I didn't intend to waste time or money with this babe, so I put together an excel spread sheet to explain my issues.

The columns read:

ROOT PROBLEMS
1. Can't keep boyfriends
2. Boredom, especially on weekends.
3. Window of opportunity closing for pregnancy

ROOT CAUSES
1. Too smart
2. Too attractive
3. Lack of good-looking, rich men

ACTIVITIES TO RESOLVE Dr. Martin,
please add your suggestions for next week. I
left a blank column for your ideas.

I knew the importance of making a good impression, so for the initial appointment, I dressed in my expensive teal silk suit to highlight my blonde hair and svelte figure. I'd just turned forty-two, but people remarked that I didn't look a day over twenty-five. I'd always taken care of myself. Had facials and got my nails done regularly. I'd even passed Mensa's IQ test although I ended up not joining. My two years as a model had taught me poise and self-confidence. My Toastmaster's group thought I was hysterically funny.

Yet I was nervous as I entered Lauren's office for my first visit. The many diplomas on the wall impressed me, and while she had a desk in her office, she sat on a beige upholstered chair beside it. I liked that I was on a matching sofa facing her and able to observe her closely.

To introduce myself, I gave Lauren a personalized business card with my name, Ashley Johnson, in calligraphy, the one I created to give to potential boyfriends or any new acquaintances. After she told me a bit about herself, I handed her the spread sheet. "I use this decision model to clarify my feelings. I like to communicate clearly."

She smiled as she scanned it. "I see," she said. I could tell she was amused, by the way she struggled to keep from laughing, but she was able to control herself. "To help you, I need to learn more about you. "Tell me about yourself," she said.

"I supervise a marketing team at Microsoft, which means I have to work a lot of overtime." I omitted the fact that I was demoted from a manager position a year ago.

Lauren nodded. "That must be difficult. There's lots of corporate stress these days in middle management."

"I understand Microsoft's business model and keep my team's productivity high." I didn't add that my boss didn't like me and that he was such a narcissist.

She looked at me with a quizzical expression. "Anything else?"

"Nope. I'm here on a mission. I want to get married, have a baby to raise with a husband, not be a single mom. I don't have much time. My last boyfriend and I broke up a year ago. A live-in toy boy who just wanted me to take care of him. I'm forty-two but tell everyone I'm thirty-six."

I decided to address her by her last name instead of Lauren to build up her ego.

"What should I do to find a *Brad Pitt* look-alike husband, Dr. Martin, someone attractive like him?"

She gave me that same quizzical look. "What does attractive mean to you, Ashley?"

"Tall and thin, not skinny but physically fit with muscles, a waist under thirty-four inches and a full head of hair. I want someone in his thirties. Someone with a future, whose paycheck is big enough to support a family if I want to quit work to be a full-time mother."

She sat back in her chair. "So love isn't that important?"

I scoffed. "Of course it is, but it comes with the package." I pointed to the spread sheet she'd laid on her desk. "Give me a plan. That's what I'm paying you for."

"Solving these problems takes time. I need to understand more about your childhood. Tell me about your mother and father, brothers and sisters."

I pointed to the spread sheet again. "I don't see siblings listed here."

She took a deep breath. "I can only help you if you're willing to explore how your past influences the way you are now."

I leaned forward. "That's bullshit. I don't have time for that. I'm interested in moving forward."

"It might seem that way, but we tend to recreate the problems we had with our primary families in our adult relationships." Frown lines spread across her forehead.

Knowing I needed to soften those frown lines for her to stay engaged, I said. "Sorry. I didn't mean that. I want to proceed.

She looked at her watch. "Good. Think about my suggestions, and we'll talk more next week."

I walked out the door, happy with the progress I had made.

The following week, I arrived early for my visit. This time I wore a lime green pantsuit with a long-sleeved ecru silk blouse. Such a contrast between Lauren's plain gray woolen suit and pink turtleneck.

Not to waste a precious minute, I began talking once I entered the room. "I only have one sister. She's jealous of me and my marketing job at Microsoft, but she's got her man. Not that I'd want my brother-in-law. He tries to hit on me all the time. Nobody knows how I struggled to get my MBA and how I worked twelve to fourteen hours every day to keep my department running smoothly. God, she has no clue."

Lauren nodded. "Lots of tension with your sister then when you were growing up?"

I nodded but looked away. I had nothing more to say.

After a long pause, she asked, "What about your parents?"

"I couldn't get along without my father. He listens to me. We talk every day on the phone. I tell Dad all about my boyfriends. He comforts me especially when we break up. He always sides with me and knows any problems aren't my fault. Dad never visits. Has that fear of going outside.

Agoraphobia, or something. Every couple months I make the three hour drive to his place."

"Uh huh. And your mother?"

"She's a little crazy and very religious. Doesn't drive, too scared. My aunt takes her everywhere. Cleans all the time. Organizes the house and Dad too. She and I don't get along."

"Do you feel your mother loves you? Any control issues with her?"

"My mother's not my problem, Dr. Martin. She's not what I came here about."

"You feel much closer to your dad then and don't think much about your mom?"

"Hell, yeah. Dad liked me best. My mother preferred my sister."

I tapped my fingers against the arm of the sofa.

"Insurance only covers one more session. I want to spend all our time on my last visit talking about finding a husband. It's the reason I'm here."

She gave me that strange look, the one that says she's frustrated but finds me appealing and interesting. She was unsure how to proceed and wondered why she took me on. I was extremely intuitive in reading people's non-verbal behavior.

When Lauren smiled, I knew she saw it my way and would follow my lead. "All right. Next time we'll only focus on the boyfriend problem."

I left the office satisfied with our progress. I liked Lauren even though I needed to keep her focused on my issues. She was probably ten years older than me but attractive in her way—smooth Mediterranean skin, toned body and a kind, energetic smile.

While dressing for my next appointment, I had to change clothes at the last minute because of a spot on my blouse and was five minutes late. After an initial greeting, Lauren asked, "What about these boyfriends then? How do you find them?" She didn't comment on my tardiness. If someone did this to me at Microsoft, I would have complained.

"The Internet. I've had my picture online, a glamour shot to get them interested. I get lots of inquiries and text the good-looking guys, take the initiative, you know. I have to sort through 300 profiles to get someone decent."

"What do you do then?"

"Talk to them on the phone, then meet in person at a restaurant, usually in the daytime. Most guys don't make it through the first screening."

"Why not, Amy?"

"Outdated photos, lies about income, bad clothes, you name it."

"What happens with the ones you keep?"

"Go out a second time. This time dinner in the evening. Then, I invite him to my house to chat and maybe watch a movie on TV. Go to bed with him two or three weeks later. Have great sex for a month and then he's outta there. Often with no real explanation—just a text, email, or nada."

Remembering the many breakups made me bite my lip in anger. To keep from screaming, I stood, pushed my chair back, and began pacing across the room.

"What are you feeling right now, Amy?"

"Dr. Martin, enough of this baloney. Pay attention. I came to you for specific advice. I don't want a listening doctor. I'm action oriented. I make things happen. I want you to be that way too. You're a nurse and a psychologist. You should understand. Tell me what to do to find a good guy. Fill out the spreadsheet I gave you. Make me a plan. A. B. C."

She broke eye contact and glanced out the window, and then looked back at me. "These problems take time to sort through."

"Nonsense. You need to work at Microsoft. Then, you wouldn't be able to sit on your butt all day and ask people questions. You'd have to produce."

"You sound angry, disrespectful even. I'll need to refer you to someone else if that continues." Her voice sounded harsh.

I sat back down on the sofa. "I'm sorry. I didn't mean to be disrespectful. It's just that I'm frustrated this process is taking so long."

She nodded. "All right, Amy. We'll do it your way for the last appointment."

I wore my Under Amour work-out clothes to the last visit, sensing Lauren wasn't impressed by my expensive outfits.

She surprised me when she said, "It's good to see you dressed casually. You seem more relaxed."

"No, I'm not more relaxed. I came here from the gym."

The rest of the visit went smoothly. Lauren was true to her word. For once she didn't ask a lot of questions. Instead she took a spread sheet from her desk and said, "Here are my ideas."

PLAN A

1. Put your profile only on one Internet site, one that's professionally managed and where the participants are screened. Maybe sign up for *It's Just Lunch*.

2. Attract men by engaging them in two-way conversations. Ask them questions about their personalities and interests. Listen to their responses.

3. Expect them to ask questions as well. Answer them honestly without overdramatizing. Don't pretend to be someone you're not.
4. Join a co-ed sports club, tennis, swimming, pickle ball. You've got so much pent-up energy.
5. Take a culinary arts or photography class. Shared activities of mutual interest are good ways to meet men.
6. Reconnect with old friends and acquaintances.

PLAN B

1. Return for more counseling to explore how childhood issues shaped your personality and way of relating to others.
2. Find another therapist to discuss your problem.

After we discussed her ideas in more depth, she said, "I hope this plan works for you. Any more questions?"

"No questions. Thanks, Dr. Martin. It took a lot to get that out of you. I'll text you the results. I know you're interested in how I make out and would like me to give you an excellent online review. It may be a few weeks."

She looked at her watch. "That's all for today, Ashley. Good luck."

***

I took Lauren's advice and reconnected with my high school and college friends. After spending weeks sifting through their suggestions of potential partners, I settled on Larry, an attorney who used to work for Microsoft before setting up his own practice.

Larry often came to Microsoft to review legal papers with my boss. I immediately noticed Larry's quick wit and youthful physique and was riveted to his azure blue eyes. Knowing my boss would have been furious at me for interrupting their business discussions, I rarely talked with Larry back then.

Larry was the complete opposite from my last boyfriend. Trevor was a happy dude who worked for a landscaping company until he lost his job for repeated tardiness. I struggled to help him develop his work ethic and even suggested he take some computer courses at the community college so he could get a job with a steadier income. He grew moody and non-cooperative and left before I kicked him out.

I took the lead with Larry and phoned him to suggest we go out for a drink the following Saturday night. He accepted the invitation and added, "Let's make it dinner, too."

Larry was a catch, thirty-seven next month but looked twenty-nine. Tall and slim with a thick head of light brown hair. And he was wealthy. That he was divorced and had two sons didn't concern me. My baby would have big brothers.

For our date, I dressed carefully in my long black silk sheath with a slit up the right side. I added a diamond pin to my hair, which I'd styled in a French twist.

Larry picked me up in his BMW convertible. I commented how handsome he looked in his charcoal gray suit and red silk tie. He must have been nervous because he hardly talked on our car ride. Instead, we listened to classical music on Sirius radio.

We sat at a small oblong table covered with a white linen tablecloth in La Parisian, one of my favorite five-star restaurants, known for its romantic ambience and gourmet food. Soft piano music played in the background. We each ordered their special, delicate Nova Scotia salmon served with sweet onions and capers. When the pianist played John Legend's "All of Me", I thought how lucky his wife, the model, Chrissy Teigen and their children were. Someday, I could have a life like theirs.

Conversation picked up after we finished a bottle of Trimbach Pinot Gris Reserve. Except for my father, never before had a man been so attentive or interested in the intricacies of my life. His questions were deep. "Did you love Trevor? How was this relationship different from your other ones?" Appearing engrossed by my answers and the feelings behind them, Larry's eyes never left mine. I almost asked the waiter to remove the two candles in the middle of the table so I could lean over to kiss him.

"I consider myself a student of human nature," he told me.

Wow, this is too good to be true, a man sensitive yet handsome and financially secure, so much more mature than Trevor. From that day on, I wanted him to be mine. I kept my father up to date on Larry and my relationship, everything except sex. Dad and I talked every evening Monday through Friday. He liked that Larry treated me with respect and was polite. I could almost see him smile over the phone. He couldn't have been happier for me.

Larry and I had a schedule; he liked predictability. At first, we saw each other only on Friday and Saturday nights. By the third week, enough time passed for us to know each other well, so I slept overnight at his place those weekends.

Later, we added Wednesdays and Sundays to our repertoire. In the beginning, it was hard for me to have such a structured relationship, but I adjusted because I loved him. I thought after three months he would ask me to move in. I suggested it would be nice for both of us. His comment, "Maybe later" left me feeling both frustrated and hopeful.

Larry liked to discuss philosophers, Thoreau, Thomas Merton, to name a few. Our Sunday morning routine was to sit in his hot tub drinking Bloody Marys. Not really interested in all that book stuff, I just listened. Even though I'd rather talk about my favorite TV shows and the newest gossip from Microsoft, I let him vent and murmured umm-hmm every so often. He smiled and hugged me tight. Sometimes, he nibbled on my ear before he kissed me.

One evening we sat at a round table at *Starbucks* sipping lattes. "I have trouble with small talk. Groups drain me. I like being with one person at a time. I'm glad it's you tonight," he said. "I didn't tell you before, but I'm seeing an online therapist. It's easier for me to talk to someone that way. He diagnosed my problem as a mild social phobia."

I squeezed his hand and kissed him on the cheek. I was glad I'd ditched Lauren, my therapist, a while back. No need for two therapists in our relationship.

I wanted to help Larry with his social phobia problem, so similar to my dad's acrophobia, which kept him homebound. Larry's issue started in sixth grade when his mother bugged him about not having playmates. I understood business-type relationships and knew Larry would respond to my gourmet dinners and open houses. "I enjoy people and am happiest at big parties. I'd love to share my acquaintances with you, in a one-to-one setting, of course," I said.

Larry looked down at the floor. "That's another issue we need to talk about. I can't handle being with new people for long stretches. I like short one-on-one conversations without social chit chat, and definitely no groups, even small ones. For sure, no strangers. I only want you."

Wow. I felt flattered he'd chosen me out of all the other people in his life.

I shuddered when Larry told me how he left his first wife, Joanna. We were back at the La Parisian, this time dining on steak béarnaise and celebrating my birthday when he said, "I couldn't stand the confinement of my marriage anymore. I took the coward's way out, had an affair. I felt bad about it, but I couldn't leave her any other way. She'd get too emotional."

I sipped my merlot.

"You didn't want to talk about problems?"

"Not the way she did. It took her hours to describe a problem I could condense into three minutes. I like to list the areas needing improvement and their possible resolutions. Then go forward from there."

"I can understand that, but you never heard her out?"

"I was too scared to talk about problems with Joanna. I couldn't handle her crying."

I twisted in my chair. "I've read in Cosmo how both partners are at fault when there's infidelity." I thought about the pain he'd caused his family and how hard it was for me when one of my old boyfriends cheated. Yet I wanted to learn more about his wife so I could better console him. "Any thought of marriage counseling?"

He shook his head. "No. I wanted out. I left her a note on the kitchen table one morning after she'd gone to work. I already had an apartment lined up that she didn't know about. The move went very smoothly; I let her keep all the furniture and only took my clothes, a few books, and my computer."

"That's terrible." I'd feel awful if it had happened to me. Poor lady. I'm more outspoken than her. He wouldn't dare treat me that way.

"It made for a nasty divorce. She took me to the cleaners."

"Oh dear."

"Joanna suggested family therapy a while back. I wasn't interested in that either."

I frowned. "Sounds as if counseling might have helped your family."

He sipped his wine. "No, the marriage was dead by then."

"What about your boys?" I asked.

"I see them every week-end and alternate holidays. They're good kids. Both are on the honor roll and the high school football team. I go to all their games. So I'm a good dad. I make sure all their needs are met."

My heart fluttered when I thought of the caring relationship Larry had with his sons. How wonderful.

"You're easy to talk with. You should be a therapist," he told me.

"I love you so much," I squeezed his hand.

Later I emailed Dr. Martin my progress. Even though I was no longer a paying patient and it had been months, I knew she'd be interested. I forgave her when she didn't respond.

One evening he talked about his affair with his secretary Kristine, who was young enough to be his daughter and his girlfriend before me. "I dated her two years before she left me. It took me several months to recover."

I stroked his cheek as he described using behavioral modification to help manage Kristine's drinking problem without going to AA or rehab. He'd only make love to her if she was sober. Larry was so smart and caring.

"Once she got her life back together, she left me. I didn't mind though. If it weren't for me, she'd still be a drunk."

Kendra was another woman in his life besides me. She was a college humanities professor, just a friend, nothing romantic. He saw her most Mondays, the one night in the week I couldn't call him unless there was a major emergency.

85

He told me they often go out to dinner at Applebee's those nights. He liked taking her to inexpensive restaurants before the crowds set in. I imagined they finish by eight; he couldn't handle talking to people longer than that. Since he took me to expensive restaurants, I knew I was special.

Larry swore he doesn't have sex with Kendra. Instead they talk about those spiritual ideas and philosophies he's so interested in. I saw magazine articles and books she'd given him to read. Maybe she knew more than I did about those topics, but I was more fun, fluffy. Larry called me his 'Little Bug'. I was jealous of Kendra. She gave Larry something I couldn't.

I wondered how she felt about Larry. My sense was she was very attracted to him but wary of his structured life and need for control. I overlooked Larry's rigid personality for the wonderful way he listened to my concerns and his skillful lovemaking.

I tried hard to please him. I was always ready for sex. I went to the beauty shop every month to highlight my hair. Larry never saw me looking sloppy; I bought most of my clothes at Nordstrom's. People said I looked good for my age; they didn't know about the work I'd had done on my face a few years back and how I worked out at the gym to keep my weight at one-twenty. I even visited his grandmother in the nursing home every week until she died

Since we'd started dating, I checked my horoscope online every morning while sipping my coffee. My mind bounced back and forth like a pinball in an arcade game when this message popped up. *This month is your lucky month. Your relationship issues will come to the forefront. Be prepared to make a serious decision.*

Does that mean Larry will ask me to marry him?

Later that week, I sat on my condo balcony meditating on my horoscope for the day, *Today will bring a big surprise.* My pinging cell phone broke my reverie. I punched connect. It was Larry. "Let's go out to dinner tonight, somewhere fancy. I have a surprise for you."

I was so excited. I dressed carefully in my black satin skirt and long-sleeved white silk blouse. I applied my make-up with precision and styled my hair in an upsweep. When he came to pick me up, I was ready.

The Chez Paul restaurant was dark, and we had a booth in the back corner. Fresh roses and candles sat in the center of our table. We ordered pinot noir and calamari for appetizers. Before we selected our entrees, Larry handed me an envelope with my name written in gold ink.

With a sheepish grin, he said, "Open your card."

With shaking fingers, I ripped the envelope. 'Happy marriage', it read. He pulled a small box from his jacket pocket and handed it to me. I opened it and gasped. "Larry, the ring's beautiful."

He smiled. "Will you marry me?"

"Oh yes," I cried. Tears filled my eyes. "I love you so much."

"I reserved a room at the penthouse in the Hilton for us. Let's go after we're done eating."

My horoscope was so right. It's my lucky day.

We spent the night making love while listening to romantic music and fell asleep wrapped in each other's arms. The next morning, I noticed his cell phone lying on the floor. When I picked it up, I accidentally pushed the *Calls Sent* button. Kendra Lewis' name popped up. The call had been placed one hour ago, while he was in the bathroom. Son of a bitch. I must act quickly. I gathered my things and slammed out the door before he finished showering. On the elevator, I slipped the ring off my finger and into my purse.

My horoscope was right. In a reverse way, it really was my lucky day. Another failure, another pothole I fell in, but I found out just in time to jump out. Plus, I had a diamond I could hawk.

I hailed an Uber to take me home. I didn't waste time checking for emails or texts from him. Instead I dropped my purse on the kitchen counter, grabbed a bottle of wine, and sat down at my computer to add 'Understand family dynamics' to my spread sheet.

Then, I phoned my neighbor for a referral to a new therapist.

Time to move on to Plan B. Maybe Lauren was right about my unresolved childhood issues.

Changing Roles

Robin, a nurse working with Doctor Green, a family practice physician, texted me. *Carol, I have an interesting case. Seventy-year-old widow needs help caring for her twenty-nine-year-old daughter with cerebral palsy recently discharged from rehab. Can you see them?*

My agency provided nursing case management to families challenged by illness and disability. Later that day, Robin came to my office to discuss Marie Holland and Haley, her daughter. My job was to coordinate an individualized long-term care plan for the family.

***

Rain pelted against my umbrella as I walked up the brick path to the Holland's small ranch home in a well-maintained neighborhood. Several white wicker chairs and clay pots of red geraniums were artfully arranged on the spacious front porch.

Marie, a heavy woman wearing black slacks and a pink sweater, welcomed me into their living room crowded with oversized furniture.

"My name's Carol Reynolds, but call me Carol. Let's sit and talk a bit." I sat down on a wing-back chair in the corner of the room. A large sofa upholstered in a pale green and yellow flowered print filled one wall. A piano, its top and bench dusty, filled the other.

"Who plays the piano?" I asked.

"Nobody's played it for years. Both Haley and I dabbled at it when she was in middle school. It's just a piece of furniture now."

Marie rubbed her knee before easing herself into a recliner across from me.

"You look tired."

"I'm exhausted. Doctor Green says I'm healthy except for high blood pressure. I take a pill every day to keep that under control and a couple Tylenol for the arthritis in my knees."

"Caregiving is exhausting. We'll talk later about ways to take care of yourself. But for now, can you tell me more about Haley?" I asked. "I see on my referral she was diagnosed with cerebral palsy as an infant, causing the muscles on her right side to be tight and stiff."

Marie sighed. "I had a horrible labor, and she was born seven weeks early. Doctor said Haley suffered a brain injury but she's not retarded. In fact, she's very smart. Her IQ was 125 when the school counselor tested her. At times, she stutters. She's always had trouble when she's nervous, but her stammer's gotten worse since she's been in rehab. Her walking and talking have never been quite right."

"Has she had a lot of therapy?" I asked.

"She's had years of therapy—physical, occupational, and speech. Lately, bending her knee became difficult, and a month ago, she fell and broke her hip. Until her fall, she worked full-time and led a nearly normal life."

I leaned forward. "So after the fall, she was in the hospital and had surgery to repair the break. Then, she was admitted to the rehab center and now she's here with you."

"I want Haley here but don't know what to do with her anymore. She's never been depressed like this and I don't have the energy I once did to care for her." Tears filled

Marie's eyes. "Just visiting her every day in the hospital and rehab center was hard. This is harder."

"Doctor Green told me Haley didn't do well in rehab."

"No, she didn't. Since she wasn't making any progress, the director wanted her moved to the facility's long-term care wing. I couldn't let that happen, so I brought her home."

"And you've always been her main caregiver?" I asked.

"My husband and I did it together until he died. I've been heartbroken since I lost Fred." She ran her fingers through her salt and pepper gray hair. "I miss him terribly. He died two years ago. Cancer." She pointed to a table with a framed photo of the three of them at Haley's high school graduation.

"A beautiful picture," I said. "You all look happy."

"The three of us got along well, but Haley was closer to him than to me. Haley always had a twinkle in her eyes for her father and made him laugh with her silly jokes. He was the bridge connecting us."

"His death must have been hard for you both." I remembered my mother's grief when my dad died and doubted I'd be any different if my husband died before me.

"Yes, Haley's a good daughter, our only child, kind of shy. She wasn't that social but had one good girlfriend in high school and was active in the photography club. Once she earned her associates degree in non-profit management, she started working at Easter Seals. She's been there nine years."

"Has she always lived with you?"

"Until last year when she moved in with her boyfriend, Jake. I've been alone since."

"That's a big change. Was it hard to see her leave?"

"Yes and no. Of course, it was difficult, but I want Haley to have an independent life. I hated to see her move in with Jake but didn't know how to stop her. She was so insistent. I could tell from the start he wasn't good enough for her. Not sure why he got involved. He's a realtor in his fifties, way too old for her and divorced. They met at a friend's wedding and dated a year before he asked her to move in. I had to adjust. Kids leaving home is part of life."

I nodded. "Sometimes we have to let our children follow their hearts. Did they get along?"

She shrugged. "For a while Haley seemed happy. She and Jake shared an interest in photography and enjoyed watching movies on his big screen TV. Beyond that, I'm not sure. She kept her office job at Easter Seals while she lived with him. She was great relating to the handicapped kids and their parents, but they let her go after the fall."

"That's too bad. When did she fall?"

"Two months ago. Haley was living with Jake when it happened. She had surgery and was in the hospital three days, then they sent her to rehab."

"It's hard to be a mother sometimes." Marie leaned forward. "Especially when your child has special needs. I'm not sure it was a good idea to have Haley move back in with me, but I want to try. It's been hard. She's been moody and withdrawn. I'm not used to that. And she's not done her exercises like she's supposed to. Says she doesn't care and that it hurts too much. The pain medicine the doctor gave her isn't helping."

"Doctors are prescribing fewer narcotics because so many have become addicted. There could be something else we can do though."

Marie nodded. "I understand about the strong drugs, but she needs relief."

"We'll figure something out," I said.

She sighed. "To top it off, Jake recently broke up with her. He came to visit her in rehab one day and told her he'd found someone else. The coward. Since then, she's hardly talked. I thought she'd perk up once she came home, but not yet."

I leaned forward in my chair. "That's a lot to deal with."

"She's gotten worse over the years, slowly mind you. First the muscle spasms, then the stiffness, and lately she's had trouble getting up from a chair or out of bed. For the most part, she's doing better here. I never noticed before, but she also has a little trouble swallowing."

A bell sounded from another room. Marie pointed to a bedroom door. "Haley wants something," she said. "She rings a bell to call me."

I stood up. "Let's go into the bedroom, so I can meet her."

Haley, a thin tall woman with short strawberry blonde hair lay in the middle of a double bed. Several framed award certificates from the Cerebral Palsy Association and childhood photos hung on the far wall. A bookcase filled with paperbacks lined another.

Haley pushed herself into a sitting position as we entered. "I heard you two talking out there and didn't want to miss anything." Her voice sounded weak.

Noting her clean flannel nightgown, I took her hand and introduced myself, then sat on an easy chair by her bed. Marie kissed her cheek and fluffed her pillow, then left us to go to the kitchen to clear up the breakfast dishes.

At first Haley answered my questions about her general health in monosyllables. Her vital signs and breath sounds were normal although she rated her hip pain as a five out of ten. Range of motion was diminished in her lower extremities and her right arm.

"How did you fall?" I asked.

She sniffled. "I slipped getting out of bed. I screamed for Jake, my boyfriend; he was in the bathroom at the time. At first, he wasn't concerned. I'd fallen several times in the past without any serious injuries. But my hip really ached and I convinced him to call 911. An ambulance rushed me to the hospital. X-rays showed I cracked the bone. The next thing I knew they wheeled me to the operating room. I woke up in the recovery room with a pin in my hip." She rubbed her right side. "Right here," she said. "Take a look how well the incision healed."

"You'll hardly have a scar in a few months. You've come a long way, Haley. How does it feel to be home?"

"I hate being stuck in my childhood bedroom. I felt like an almost-normal woman living with Jake. Now I feel like I'm fifteen again."

"I get that. But you want to be here now. Right?"

"I couldn't stand the rehab center. The noise, the food, the bad TV channels, my roommate and all her visitors drove me crazy. Then, Jake wouldn't take me back. It all brought me down. Thank God my mother could take me in."

"You sound sad."

"Yeah, I'm discouraged, depressed even. It's all overwhelming."

"I can understand why you feel that way. It can take a while to get back into your old routines. We need to make a plan and get some help in here."

Haley nodded. "Yeah, there's a lot to think about."

"Let's start with getting you out of bed."

"Since the fall, I've been afraid to get out of bed without help."

"It's smart to ask for help, at least for a while." I called for Marie to come back to the bedroom and taught her how to steady Haley's walker so that she could safely transfer from the bed to a nearby chair. "What's next?" she asked once she was seated.

"I'll make sure a physical therapist is here tomorrow and the occupational and speech therapists next week. And I'll contact the doctor about the pain and ask him to consider an anti-depressant. What about a home health aide to help with showering and bed making?"

"That sounds all right. I'll try anything to feel better," Haley said.

Marie, now standing by her chair, agreed. She smiled as she gazed at Haley. "You've talked more this morning than the last two days." Tears filled her eyes as she took my hand. "It's a miracle. Thank you, Carol."

***

After being on the new medications for three weeks, Haley's pain level had dropped to a two and her mood had lightened. Marie enjoyed doting on Haley and keeping her amused, a bittersweet labor of love that exhausted her at the end of the day. The extra attention improved Haley's emotional outlook but at the same time made her more dependent and needy.

One day while Haley rested in her bedroom, Marie and I sat on the porch talking about Marie's health. While her blood pressure remained in the normal range, I counseled her that if she overextended herself too much, she could become ill. I also feared Marie's doting would encourage unhealthy dependence for them both.

It was time for her to find a diversion, something fun to pass the time. I thought about the piano sitting in the living room. "What about getting back into music? Let's go inside and give it a try. Your piano is waiting for you to play it," I said.

Marie smiled. "I've thought about it but I'm too rusty. The three of us used to play. I did save some sheets of my favorites. They're under the bench seat."

"Let's pull them out. You can play for me. I have a tin ear so won't know whether it's good or bad."

We walked into the living room, and, with my encouragement, she sat down and played. I stood beside her. Minutes later Haley rang her bell, and Marie stopped playing. We went to the bedroom to find Haley halfway out of bed. "Whoa," I exclaimed.

"I want to join you. You're leaving me out of the fun."

For the next twenty minutes, Marie and her daughter pounded the piano keys. The music certainly wasn't melodic, but it warmed my heart to see the two of them willing to engage in an activity they'd enjoyed in the past. Playing the piano provided an enjoyable way for Haley to exercise her fingers, which improved the strength and muscle tone in her hands.

Knowing that a consistent exercise program would help prevent loss of muscle mass and premature aging, I spent my next several visits reinforcing the various therapists' suggestions for transferring, muscle strengthening, and safe ambulation. A speech therapist gave Haley jaw, lip, and tongue exercises, which improved the clarity of her speech. She taught her how to use a mirror to gain facial control and ways to improve her swallowing. Another exercise was blowing a whistle, the kind referees use at sporting events. She and I each had one, and we had contests to see who could whistle the longest. Haley loved to win, and often I let her.

Those days Marie spent the hour on the porch. "You two drive me crazy," she laughed.

I educated Haley about her medications and suggested home modifications to make the home safer. Marie agreed to install grab bars in the bathroom shower and railings on each side of the steps from the house to the garage.

On one of my visits, Marie answered the door with tears in her eyes. "I'm missing Fred big time today. It would have been our forty-fifth anniversary, and here I am alone."

We sat in the living room to talk. She looked at the family photo on the end table, then reached for an album on the coffee table. After we spent an hour looking at the photos, she said, "I need to do something outside the house."

We discussed support groups. With my encouragement, she agreed to attend a bereavement support group meeting at a nearby church.

An afternoon a few weeks later, she and I sat at her kitchen table drinking coffee. "Talking with the bereavement group members is comforting. Gosh, there are so many people like me," Marie said. "So many widows grieving their husbands. We talked a lot about caregiving, too. Many mentioned feeling helpless to make things better for their loved ones. I can understand that. I dealt with those feelings with Fred and now Haley."

I poured cream in my coffee and helped myself to one of her homemade oatmeal raisin cookies.

"We all have had to adjust to living alone." She hoisted up the waistband of her slacks. "I miss having someone next to me when I go to bed. I can't imagine sleeping with another man. This old body of mine is going to the dogs. I'm embarrassed just thinking about anyone seeing my sags and wrinkles, yet it would be pleasant to have a man around."

"Anyone in particular?" Many women, young and old, have self-image issues. Haley and Marie aren't the only ones.

She smiled. "There is a widower about my age in the group. Gene's his name. He talked about losing his wife to cancer and also about not being able to save his son who died in an auto accident."

"You two have something in common then."

She sighed. "I told him that I wished I could do more for my daughter. But there's nothing more I can do. She has to live the life she was dealt, knowing I'll always love and support her."

I squeezed her hand. "You're right, and I think Haley knows that."

"I suppose," Marie said. "She's doing better. She rarely rings the bell to alert me anymore. Her mood has definitely improved. She's even back to joking around once in a while."

I set down my coffee mug next to Marie's. "The physical therapist and I have her walking with a cane now, and she's often sitting on the porch when I visit. Soon she'll be showering independently." I was pleased to see the improvement in Haley's mobility, as physical health and emotional health are interrelated.

During several visits, Haley and I sat on wing back chairs in her bedroom talking about her boyfriend. "I cry a lot over Jake. He cheated on me and then dumped me because I'm handicapped. Yet I could keep up with him with all our activities."

I shook my head. "I doubt your handicap was the only reason. Probably withdrawing is how he deals with relationship issues in general. I wish you two could have talked more about your deeper feelings."

"Jake wasn't good about feelings. He didn't ask personal questions or want to know my inner workings." Tears filled her eyes. "Every day I hate my body, and I sure don't want to talk about that. If I were normal, I'd be married and have two kids by now."

"Maybe yes, maybe no," I said. "You learned a lot about yourself being with Jake."

Haley nodded. "I should have talked more about how my needs are different because of my cerebral palsy."

"That's true, but relationships are about communication whether you're disabled or not." I thought of the break-ups in my own life. Many physically healthy couples have trouble maintaining intimate relationships, and it's even harder for those living on society's fringe.

"Even though you shouldn't try to hide it, your disability doesn't define you. You're a unique person in your own right."

"Jake never loved me for who I am." Tears ran down her cheeks. "He visited me every day the first week I was in rehab. But the following week, when he came in with a bouquet of flowers, I knew something was wrong. He never gave me gifts, let alone flowers."

"What happened?"

"He started off saying I couldn't come back to the condo, that he'd fallen out of love with me and was seeing someone else. The relationship was becoming too burdensome. Said he wasn't the partner I needed. It shocked the hell out of me."

"I can't imagine. Your broken hip was his *out* then," I said.

"Anyway, I threw the flowers at him and told him to leave. Then I sobbed and sobbed so long the doctor had to give me medicine to quiet me."

"I'm sorry this happened, but I'm glad you didn't beg Jake to come back."

I squeezed her shoulder.

"I've had boyfriends before but the relationships didn't last longer than several months, and we never lived together. My first boyfriend one was in high school and we never had real sex. Even though we broke up, the memory of being loved by someone comforts me." I lost myself making love to Jake. It made me feel whole."

Over the next weeks, Haley talked more about her struggles to find a partner. "I'm nervous when I meet men. Jake was nice in bed at first. It felt wonderful. For once I was a normal woman. Then kaput. The lovemaking was over almost before it started. Now I wonder if it was my stiff movements during sex or if he left because I sometimes needed my walker or cane. Even having to wear my orthopedic shoes instead of high heels when we went out could have bothered him. Maybe he didn't like my stutter."

Haley shared how many promising relationships turned to friendships and how efforts to minimize her disability backfired in the end. She wanted to marry and have children but worried about pregnancy and her ability to care for them.

"I learned from all this that I need to love myself more if I'm ever going to have a healthy relationship with a man. When I eventually find one, I'll be honest about my limitations. That's what I'm going to work on—loving myself and feeling comfortable in my body. Everything's harder when you're disabled. After that, I may put a profile up on eHarmony or find a photography group to join.

"That all makes sense. A counselor I work with specializes in clients with disabilities. She has cerebral palsy, too. Her name's Janice. Would you like to talk to her?"

Haley took a deep breath. "Gosh. I don't know. I could give it a try. Maybe since she's also handicapped, she'd understand me."

One month later, Haley and I sat on the porch. She'd agreed to work long term with Janice and see her once a week. "She's helping me come to terms with my disability and learn to adjust my expectations. We've talked about other things, too—like how much I want to have my own place but at the same time feel bad about leaving Mom. I worry. She lost her get-up-and-go after Dad died."

I sighed. "The future is hard to predict, but you have options. So does your mother. I think your mom would be fine with you staying with her. On the other hand, each of you has your own challenges to deal with. Sometimes, taking care of ourselves is a welcome gift to our families."

"I appreciate Mom's caring and in some ways she needs me here, but I must move ahead with my life. I feel like a child living here."

"It's hard to get out of that child role sometimes, but it's important." I paused. "There are apartments in supervised independent living communities. Another option is group homes where six to twelve residents have their own bedrooms but share the other living space. Perhaps, you could even manage a small regular apartment on your own."

We talked in detail about the pros and cons of each. "I'm not sure what I want to do. They're all good ideas. Money could be a problem though," Haley said.

Two weeks later, she greeted me with good news. "I contacted Easter Seals. I had to go in and meet with the director. They are giving me my job back. She said my talking has improved. When I told Janice, I wanted to work more with the preschoolers one-on-one, she encouraged me to talk to the Easter Seals director about it. I did and they are willing to train me to be an occupational therapy aide. That means a lot. Transportation won't be a problem. I have the Ford Escape my parents bought for me modified with all the adaptive equipment I need. I've been driving a bit the last couple weeks to get used to the car again."

"That's wonderful," I said. "I'm happy for you. You have a lot going for you and a lot to think about. We'll talk more next time."

As I was leaving the house, Marie followed me to the front door. "Let's walk out to the porch to talk," I suggested.

She sat down on the wicker rocker and motioned me to do the same. Marie hesitated before speaking. "I'm worried there will be no one to care for Haley after I die. I probably have five or so more years in me to take care of her, and then what? I'm thinking about a group home for her, one close so we can see each other a lot." She blushed. "Gene suggested that idea to me. We've been meeting for lunch every now and again."

I smiled, pleased she'd found a man she'd felt comfortable with. "He sounds like a good friend."

She shrugged. "Yes, perhaps he'll become more than a friend. Who knows? Regardless I've already told him Haley comes first, and he understands that."

I nodded. "It's ironic. Just this afternoon Haley told me she also was concerned about the future. We talked a lot about her options. She even asked questions about a nearby group home, one with twelve residents."

"What a coincidence. Gene and I visited it last week. A private bedroom's available if she wants it. I feel guilty not talking about it to her first and now suggesting it."

"A possible solution, and it's better late than never. It's Haley's decision. At this point, she can function pretty well independently," I said.

Marie clutched the arm of her chair. "She has a small disability check, and Fred left money for her in a special needs trust. If there's a shortfall or an emergency, I could help her with her bills." She tapped her fingers on a nearby side table.

I smiled. "We've made a lot of progress. Why don't you two go to the group home this week and see what she thinks?"

***

The following week, the three of us sat around the kitchen table. With quivering lips, Haley said, "Mom took me to the group home and showed me a typical room. Some people there are up and about and just need a little help with transportation. Everyone has as much freedom as they can handle but a few are more disabled than me. A few even need wheelchairs to get around."

Marie smiled. "I was happy you seemed to like it there. It's safe and nearby."

Haley stammered. "I've been thinking more about the group home and realize it's not for me. Not yet, anyway. I'm thinking of a one-bedroom apartment in town close to the grocery store and doctor's offices. She looked at Marie. "I just found out that Easter Seals is going to train me to work with the kids."

"They are? That's wonderful news. A big relief. I know how bored you were there handling the paperwork," Marie exclaimed.

"Haley's doing so well and wants to be as independent as possible," I said to encourage her to express her feelings.

"You're sure about living alone in an apartment?" Marie asked. "What if you fall?"

"The physical and occupational therapists say my leg muscles are stronger and that, if I keep up my exercises, I shouldn't fall. Plus there are so many apps I can use to get services without leaving my building. And I promise to wear an emergency alert bracelet and carry my cell phone all the time."

Marie ran her fingers across her forehead. "I liked the security the group home provided, but I think you're right to stretch a bit and see what happens. No matter what, I'll always be here for you."

Memories of taking my eighteen-year-old son to college and helping him set up his dorm room flashed through my mind. Even now I sensed those feelings of excitement, sadness, and satisfaction. Like me, Marie was about to face a milestone where the parent-child relationship changes.

Haley nodded. "Thanks, Mom." She wiped a tear from her face. "A regular apartment is the best choice for me and for you, as well. I'm not going to even have a half-normal life unless I learn how to live alone. Carol and Janice agree I need to get situated now." Her voice cracked as she looked at Marie. "You need to promise you'll hire a housekeeper to help out two or three times a week."

Marie laughed. "So you're turning the tables on me?"

Haley smiled. "Yep. It's fair game. Give a little. Take a little."

I leaned forward. "I agree. It's wise to start getting used to some paid housekeeping help to give you more time for things you enjoy."

The hard lines between Haley's eyes had softened. A soft smile tinged her lips. She looked at Marie. "You deserve a few quiet years. You and Dad have taken care of me all my life. You deserve the freedom to do things your way, and I deserve a chance to be who I am and learn to overcome the scary feelings about being disabled."

Marie bit her lip. "Now that you mentioned your good news, I want to share mine. I've met a gentleman at my support group. We've gotten together for lunch a few times. We're just friends." Marie's serious expression signaled how difficult this conversation was for her.

Haley chuckled. "I'm glad you found someone you like."

Marie blushed. "My wish is that you have the best life possible, and you know what that is better than I do. You've been a gift to Dad and me, and you'll always come first." She paused. "I'll miss you tons. I plan to visit you real often in your new place, wherever that is."

Haley reached over and squeezed Marie's arm. "Hope it's not too often, Mom. I need to learn to live on my own."

Marie smiled. "We can get together some evenings and watch Netflix movies like we used to. I'll buy you a portable piano for a housewarming gift. You seem to like playing these last few weeks."

"Wow, Mom, thank you."

Marie bit her lip again. "I'll cook a fancy dinner some Sundays. Something to look forward to all week. Of course, you'll come on the holidays and on your birthday. Other than that, I'll bow out."

Haley laughed. "Hearing that is a good start. It's hard for me to say no to all your offers of help. What about you coming to my apartment sometime and letting me cook?"

"I'd like that," Marie said.

Haley squeezed her mother's hand.

Marie looked at me. "I've been praying for a solution, one I could feel good about, and now we have it. Thank you."

Haley leaned forward and hugged Marie. "Maybe my fall has been a gift to all of us."

I smiled. "Yes. Often gifts can come from unexpected places and lead to new beginnings."

Spam, Anyone?

With the bank about to foreclose on his multi-million-dollar mansion in the Hamptons, Samuel Shiner was worried. As CEO of Health Care Spam Inc., an international online marketing agency based in New York City but with offices throughout the United States, he was held responsible for several of his major pharmaceutical and cosmetic companies cancelling their advertising contracts. They blamed HCS for a lack of demand for their products. Samuel was desperate to make up the shortfall and anxious to restore his stellar reputation as a main player in Internet commerce.

Early in his tenure at HCS, Samuel insisted the entire staff use nicknames to protect their confidentiality and maintain their autonomy. At a staff luncheon one year, a waitress called Samuel, Sleazy Sam. Even though he initially rebelled, the name stuck. Staff continued to call him Sam to his face but used Sleazy Sam when he wasn't around.

Sleazy called an emergency meeting of his upper management staff to present his solution to HCS's canceled contracts. Once the three top managers were settled around the circular boardroom table, Sleazy stroked his gray beard, then tapped his fingers on the table to get their attention. "The company's in trouble. We need to increase HCS's sales revenue by ten percent before the auditors discover we're operating in the red." He spoke slowly; the words poured from his mouth like honey dripping from a spoon.

Sleazy stared at his managers—Victor Vee, Bertha Bee, and Dolly Dee, each one responsible for supervising fifty independent contractors working online, mostly in third world countries. Victor's team focused on prescription medications. Bertha led the group responsible for beauty products, and Dolly handled the division of diet drugs to promote weight loss.

Sleazy laid his iPad on the table. "I'm instituting an e-mail marketing contest among your three teams. I expect each of your team members to submit ten creative slogans or new marketing techniques. I will select two winners next month. Each of them will receive a year's supply of our health care products. Naturally, I'll use the free samples we get from our vendors."

Victor Vee, a thin man who wheezed when under stress, said "We have to give 'em more than that." He wiped sweat from his brow and bald head.

"Nonsense," said Sleazy. "People love facial hydrating creams, the anti-aging vitamins, and the fat-burning elixirs we sell. The contest will begin today and last for four weeks. I expect you and all of our workers to participate."

Bertha Bee, a forty-year-old single mom, twirled strands of her shoulder-length blonde hair, brittle from her years' use of HCS hair coloring products. "So we're competing against each other? That will cause friction between us. Not a good idea."

Sleazy cleared his throat. "Competition for a worthwhile prize is a strong motivator. My goal is to increase the number of internet users who download HCS advertisements and buy our vendors' goods, and I want all three of you to demand each independent contractor on your team to submit ten original ideas. In addition to keeping up their normal workload, of course."

Bertha twisted in her chair and bit her lip before speaking. "I refuse to force extra work on my people. I want to keep our three-person management team intact."

Sleazy leaned forward. "I will not tolerate dissention among any of our employees, including you three. I expect you all to keep a civil environment. You'll be let go if you don't comply."

Bertha looked down and tore a loose thread from her blouse.

Victor squeezed his plastic bottle of HCS vitamin water. "No way we can do that," he said between breaths. "My workers are taxed to the max already." He gasped. He'd hoped his plans to retire next year wouldn't be compromised. His wife had complained for years that Victor's low salary didn't allow them enough money to achieve their greatest dream, moving to Arizona and building a ranch home there.

Sleazy pointed his finger at each of them in turn and spoke in a harsh tone. "Sounds as if you care more about your team members than the company's profits. My plan is more than fair. An extra prize will be a random HCS gift card given to a select few of our better workers. The project is a win-win. The gift card winners will buy our products, thus increasing sales. We'll also get extra work out of the teams without raising wages."

"But what about us?" asked Dolly Dee. "We're overworked, too." She took a sip of her diet soda, praying the meeting would end soon, so she wouldn't miss her mani-pedi spa appointment. Dolly, nearly thirty pounds overweight, lived with her dog, Puddles, in a one-bedroom Manhattan apartment. Still single at thirty, she dreamed to marry someday and move to the suburbs.

Sleazy pulled a comb from his shirt pocket and slicked back his hair. "All right. I'll sweeten the pot. One of you will receive a five-hundred-dollar bonus as the winning team manager." He looked at his watch. "I have five minutes to hear from each of you on how your teams will proceed."

The three managers sat up straighter and immediately looked at Sleazy and then at each other. "V Team has amazing drug ads," said Victor. "Vigora for erectile dysfunction, Valient for anxiety, and Vicodino for pain. We use pop-ups to push our medications and personalize our e-mail with the computer owner's name and force them to listen to audio messages. Omitting or minimizing the drugs' side effects will make us the winner."

"B Team has the best ads for beauty and other vanity products," said Bertha. "Botox, belly liposuction, and baldness balms. We appeal to emotions. Our spam has music in the background and focuses on youthful bodies without having to exercise. With some better photography, we can beat you both." She spat her words out in an angry staccato.

Dolly shook her head. "D Team has the most awesome diet compound ads. Diet doughnuts, draft beer, and date bars. We encrypt our message subliminally; improving the embedded images of food and people eating in fancy restaurants will be our strategy. Don't count us out."

Sleazy yawned. "I've heard enough to know that you all get the idea. "Spread the word about the contest to the teams, all the peons from Nigeria, China, and India. Text, phone, or e-mail them—whatever. Remind our third world country workers that the masses are all looking for an enhanced sex life and a svelte body. People are the same all over the world. The meeting's adjourned." He stood up and left the room.

For a minute, the managers sat speechless until Dolly said, "Sleazy's back at it, putting pressure on us to do the impossible. No morals, that man."

"I agree. He doesn't give a rat's ass about us or our team members," added Victor.

Bertha cleared her throat. "I support Sleazy. We need the work, and the pay is enough to keep a roof over our heads. We have to do our best. You heard Sleazy. The company could go bankrupt, and then what will we do?" She didn't mention the extra bonus she received every year for the overnights they'd spent together.

After much complaining and the added five-hundred-dollar incentive, the managers agreed to move ahead, each group expecting to come out the winner.

***

Spam e-mailer Eddie from Calcutta received the directive from Victor, his manager, and was so angry he smashed his fist on his computer and cracked the casing. He could hardly feed his children on the one-hundred-forty rupees an hour that he earned. Fortunately, his wife's work as an aide at the children's school supplemented his meager wage. Even with the two incomes, the family of five could only afford a small two-bedroom home. For months, Eddie had begged Victor for a pay raise to compensate for the required unpaid overtime. After all, he'd worked for HCS for twelve years in a one room manufactured hut with a simple metal desk and chair. The only perk was up-to-date Internet and Wi-Fi access.

Eddie had covered the room's bare walls with posters of Deepak Chopra and Dinesh D'Souza. On his half-hour lunch break, he watched American movies on his iPad and read books by Salman Rushdie and Arundhati Roy. He'd styled his dark hair in neat spikes like he'd seen on an American YouTube video. His dream was to send his children to an American university to learn business strategies to bring back to Calcutta.

Eddie wasn't as dumb as Victor and Sleazy thought. He'd learned a lot about hacking online accounts and had assembled a complete mailing list of Sleazy's contacts. With sweat pouring from his brow, he sat staring at his computer deciding how to proceed. He fingered the ring in his right ear and then lit a Benson and Hedges cigarette. Sleazy's expectations were unfair. Now was the time to act.

Eddie pulled up his spread sheet on his laptop and e-mailed his complaint about Sleazy's new directive to the entire e-mailing crew worldwide. "I'm organizing a union. We e-mail spammers should not be working for minimum wage. I already changed my name from Rajeev to Eddie to sound American and took a course in conversational English to please Sleazy. Enough is enough! Sleazy should pay for the time we put into creating these extra advertisement ideas. Sign the petition below if you agree."

Ninety-five percent of HCS's workers signed the petition, and Eddie sent it to Sleazy. The health care spam czar called another emergency meeting with his directors, Victor, Bertha, and Dolly, threatening to reduce the wages of HCS's entire work force or lay off twenty percent of the employees unless his demands were met.

Eddie and his peon worker group, now calling itself SOS (Spoilers of Spam) remained firm and organized an e-mail spam strike determined to undermine Sleazy's contest directive by decreasing HCS's contracts even further. The pop-up blockers and spam filters they put on all the world's computers immobilized Sleazy's hard drive. His e-mail attempts to demote or fire the workers failed. He couldn't get the message through and had to resort to snail mail to send out the pink slips.

As the weeks passed, the SOS became more committed to the cause and organized a worldwide spam strike. Only a few, like Sparetire Seth and his roommate, Bellyfat Bill, workers on Dolly's team in the Philippines, became scab spammers. Victor and Bertha complained of favoritism to Sleazy to no avail.

A splinter spam union group was organized to ambush Sparetire and Bellyfat by throwing cans of the old-fashioned Spam at their house. Sparetire and Bellyfat, who lived together in a trailer park in the Florida Panhandle, didn't care. They opened the cans and gorged on the meat, either between slabs of bread or mixed with fried eggs. The two gained weight, enough to classify them as severely obese. Neighbors complained about the mountain of rusty tins behind their mobile home and hired a seedy lawyer to file a civil lawsuit and represent them in court. In the end, a judge sentenced Sparetire and Bellyfat to have their yard cleaned up within the week and perform seventy-five hours of community service serving spam at a local soup kitchen.

Chynna Ling, nicknamed Singalong Sue, an HCS worker from Beijing who also worked the night shift in a hospital as a nurses' aide, contacted Eddie. "The stress from working sixty hours a week e-mailing Sleazy's spam messages is how I got hooked on Valient. Let's get all the nurses behind us. They're the most honest professional group in the world. Nurses are committed to the health and wellbeing of the population worldwide. They know medical spam is not in the best interests of the people. We need to educate them on what's going on. They work so hard taking care of patients they don't have time to keep up with the growing spam technology."

Singalong, realizing that the nurses in her country played a critical role in global health care, wrote to the heads of the various nursing organizations in the United States. While altruism was her main motivator, she wanted to highlight the poor salaries and working conditions of nurses in Beijing and the rest of China. Her nurse friends who worked in the ICU of a large urban hospital had heavy patient loads and worked long hours, twelve hour shifts three to four times a week plus mandatory overtime. The children's wards were particularly stressful as parents usually had only one child and were heavily invested in them. They reacted violently to medical errors or expensive medical procedures gone awry.

Singalong understood her job at HCS was easier and her salary higher than her cohorts who worked in hospitals. By joining the spam group, she could help them organize a trade union.

The nurses in the United States spread SOS's message online, formed a PAC (political action committee), and organized petition drives. They highlighted their cause with e-mails and letters to the local newspapers and congressional leaders and flooded TikTok, Twitter, Facebook, Instagram, MeWe, and Parler accounts with SOS's message.

The Senate's majority leader, Carl Cozener, made deals with his party's members to support the SOS agenda. They clashed with Fred Flimflammer and his minority group of opposing senators. Each party had several multi-billion-dollar corporations' support behind it, causing a stalemate in Congress. Members from the House of Representatives faced a similar problem. Both sides faced pressure from their constituents to make a decision.

Citizens' groups of both parties used social media to publicize their platform. They used television, Twitter, and YouTube videos to promote their ideas. They held public protests, which, at times, resulted in rioting in major cities. Backlash against health-related spam intensified. Some states called in the National Guard to quell the unrest. The attorney general authorized the FBI to further investigate.

Affected by Spam (ABS) support groups sprung up across the nation to handle peoples' anxiety and distress. Subtypes of the group focused on ABS Enablers (ABSE) and ABS Aggressors (ABSA).

After finding no relief from ABSA's anger management tutorial, Sleazy became so distraught he asked Victor to find him Valient online so he could sleep at night and function throughout the day. Then his lower back began to ache, so Victor obtained Vicodin to relieve the pain. To deal with Sleazy's erratic behavior, Scarlett, a longtime girlfriend known for her carrot red hair, tried the ABSE's tutorial to no avail and left him to move in with Sparetire and Bellyfat.

Now Sleazy spent his days in bed watching television and playing video games. He lost muscle mass and gained weight. His skin became flabby. Bertha arranged a belly liposuction. He cursed when he saw the footage of Scarlett, Sparetire, Bellyfat, and Singalong on television and YouTube videos. Dolly brought him diet draft beer and thanked God the high alcohol content calmed him.

The United States Department of Justice responded to the nurses' PAC demands and appointed a special counsel to investigate Sleazy's financial affairs, using millions of taxpayer dollars to pay for the seven member panel. The Attorney General announced the committee's findings in a short prime time television appearance on all the major news stations.

Next, the AG scheduled a news conference. He stood in an auditorium in front of the American flag and in a forceful voice stated, "The Department of Justice is charging Samuel S. Shiner, also known as Sleazy Sam, with hiding money illegally in overseas investments. He has amassed millions over the years."

The FBI arrested Sleazy and charged him with mail fraud and money laundering but released him on a $500,000 bond. Victor, Bertha, and Dolly were offered immunity if they would testify. Bertha and Dolly agreed to participate. Victor declined but hired his own personal attorney.

Tweets on the topic reached an all-time high in a matter of minutes. The BBC and Asian networks picked up the story, and it spread worldwide in hours. Charges against the three managers were eventually dropped. The AG recommended that e-mail spam advertising of health care products be outlawed throughout the United States.

Sleazy became more and more incapacitated and reclusive. HCS's debt skyrocketed paying for all his on-line medications and other health care products. When his liposuction site became infected, Victor bought him the antibiotic, vancotoxin, online. The medication affected Sleazy's kidneys, and they shut down. An acute respiratory virus, ARV.doc, further complicated his condition. Sleazy died days later with Bertha and Dolly by his side. Scarlett was nowhere to be found. His death certificate read *spam related staph infection and ARV.doc pneumonia.*

The CDC (Center for Disease Control) conducted a study to identify and isolate the ARV virus and offered grants for independent researchers to study the problem. Several universities took up the challenge. The World Health Organization (WHO) organized its own committees for an international investigation. Eventually the United Nations became involved.

In a close vote, the United Nations declared health care spam an international crime, all thanks to Eddie, Singalong, and the nurses. People around the world rejoiced. Eddie cajoled WHO to establish a fund for the HSC employees to cover their strike expenses and provide job placement and retraining. Soon most of the world's population knew about the fund and the site to send their money to: SOS c/o WHO 1 Disk Drive USB Port Geneva, Switzerland.

Donations drifted in from all over the world.

***

Governments worldwide developed cost constraints to prohibit gouging by pharmaceutical companies but allowed them enough capital to cover the cost of research into new therapeutics.

Eddie established a non-profit agency, similar to the states' Habitat for Humanity, to improve the housing situation in Calcutta. He also set up a non-profit scholarship fund to pay for select Indian students' education in America.

Singalong turned her efforts into providing union representation for nurses at two of the largest Beijing hospitals. She expanded her role as a SOS advocate to include ways to improve patient care and overall health. Her expertise and willingness to travel throughout China and sharing her knowledge on nutrition, exercise, and health management earned her a nomination for the Nobel Peace Prize.

Victor retired to find that he was no longer wheezing. He and his wife, who had managed their assets well, moved to an upscale condo in Phoenix, close to a golf course, restaurants, and shopping. To make up to Eddie for allowing Sleazy to take advantage of him and his Calcutta group over the years, he donated two thousand dollars to his non-profit educational start-up.

Dolly set up a non-kill animal shelter in the city and devoted her time to animal welfare, particularly advocating for abused dogs and cats. She was instrumental in obtaining felony convictions for those who mistreated them and added three more rescue dogs to her household.

Bertha and Scarlett took a different approach. They changed their names and joined a group of hackers active on the dark Web who weaseled their way into the credit card

116

accounts of unsuspecting customers. Their technical expertise allowed their nefarious ways to go unchallenged.

Sparetire and Bellyfat tried to organize a scab group to break the nurses' unions Singalong had established. Since they had gained so much weight during the year, they lacked the physical stamina to follow through successfully. They took their failure in stride and moved to California to join a hippie commune, *The Brotherhood of the Sun.*

***

Later in the year, the front page of the *New York Times* featured the success of SOS with individual stories about the participants. The journalist ended the article with the following comment: chaos and unrest—it always brings about change and gives us examples of mankind's best and worst behaviors.

The Hamster's Wheel

The police pull me over on the highway and accuse me of speeding. The God damn cops make me get out of my car, tell me I've been weaving in and out of traffic, then ask me a lot of questions and force me to take a breath test. "You're under arrest," they say.

When I tell one of them to 'go to Hell' and try to kick him, he handcuffs me, stuffs the boys and me in a patrol car, and drives us to the police station.

From there, I go to jail and the boys to my sister's. As they take my boys away, seven-year-old Cole screams, "Mommy, Mommy." My Ben is brave. He turns his head to the side, but doesn't cry out, maybe because he's two years older.

I sit alone in the jail cell until a fat lady with dull brown hair and wearing a navy-blue police uniform unlocks the door and ambles in. She makes me take off all of my clothes and checks me for drugs and other contraband.

The bitch, whose name tag reads Officer Carlow, gives me an orange jump suit. "You'll get a clean one every other day," she says.

She makes me fill out and sign a bunch of papers. Then, she leads me through several hallways and unlocks the door to another big room with long tables in the middle and a dozen cots lined against the wall. Before she leaves, she points out which bunk is mine. A group of crazy women, also wearing those orange suits, snicker when I almost trip on a magazine left on the floor. I give them the finger. I want to go home, back to my apartment and my boyfriend, Teddy. He gets me the drugs I need to stay sane.

The next day, a lady guard comes in the big room after we'd finished lunch, a tuna sandwich and potato chips served on paper plates, tasteless food we had to stand in line and wait fifteen minutes to get. "You have a two o'clock court appearance," she says. "Hold out your legs so I can put the shackles on."

While the bitch chains my ankles, I want to slap her across the face but have learned from the others that will only get me more time, so I take a deep breath and do what she asks.

She leads me to a parking garage and pushes me into the back of a van with several other women I've never seen. After a short drive, they drop me off at the rear door of the courthouse. A cute young deputy, with blond hair and a warm smile walks me in. I shuffle along because of the chains on my ankles. In my better days, I'd have made a pass at him.

I get to spend two minutes with my lawyer, a skinny nerd dressed in a gray suit who introduces himself as Joe Johnson. We sit on a bench against the hallway wall outside the courtroom. He flips through a stack of papers in his briefcase while I tell him my story. He cuts me off in the middle of a sentence. "Crystal, we need to move into the courtroom. The judge will ask how you plead, guilty or not. I suggest "not guilty." We'll try for rehab instead of jail."

"Rehab? What does that mean?"

"Better deal than jail," he says. "Come on. The judge gets mad if he has to wait."

I feel engulfed in a black cloud as I follow him through the big doors. Men and women are seated on the wooden benches in the back of the room. Most of the people are quiet; several are whispering to one another.

Joe and I have to stand before a judge, who is dressed in a preacher-like black robe. He sits behind a huge, elevated desk and stares down at me with a piercing high-and-mighty look. The nerd lawyer talks so fast I can't understand what he is saying.

As the judge rambles off two charges against me, *DUI on the freeway with minor children in the car*, and *driving with a suspended license*, he runs his fingers through his short gray hair. His stare turns into a frown. "How do you plead?" he asks.

"Not guilty," I say.

Joe clears his throat. "Your honor, Will you consider dropping the charges if Crystal agrees to be admitted to a treatment facility?"

Under his breath, I hear the judge sigh, "Another one." I hope I heard wrong.

The judge agrees to send me to drug rehab center. "You're lucky. Make the best of this opportunity. You won't get a second chance." He pounds his desk with a little wooden hammer. "We'll see you back here in a month to reassess the situation."

It's over just like that.

The same van that brought me to the courthouse drives me to the drug rehab center, Harvest Home, a dilapidated two-story wooden frame house with ten rooms and housemothers watching over us around the clock. At the center, I have my own small pale green room with a single bed and scratched wooden dresser. A stupid picture of a man in a red jacket riding a black horse through the woods hangs on the wall across from my bed. I've never seen a real horse or a man dressed in red.

Why don't they hang a poster of my favorite band, Metallica, or something else I'd recognize?

It seems life should be better at the treatment center, being away from all the crazy women and not having to wear the orange suit, but that's when the panic sets in. The first time it wakes me up is at three A.M.

The nightmare feeling happens more often and can come on any time, even when it is daylight out, often suddenly when I'm scared and upset, this feeling always the same, no matter what I'm doing, or whom I'm with. I've changed into someone I don't recognize, not the brash and brave Crystal Walker I always thought was me but a nervous and unsure excuse for a woman. Now I have no Vicodin or wine and beer to keep me calm. At first, I needed the pills for the bad pain in my back. Months later, I needed them just to survive.

***

Many nights, I wake up in a cold sweat. I've turned into a dark brown hamster with beady eyes racing on an exercise wheel. My heart races. My breaths come in pants, short, rapid and erratic. The inside of my head turns into a hollow empty cavern. I feel as if I'm dying. The hamster's face fades and becomes my face. I can't erase the image from my mind.

In the nightmare, I'm no longer Crystal Walker, once a housekeeper in a nursing home but a miniature woman running ahead of the beady-eyed rodent over the metal spokes.

The hamster is chasing my two boys and me. The wheel is spinning; the whirling sound shatters my eardrums. I run faster and faster to keep up. My toes catch on the spokes. I fall. I am lying on the bottom of the cage. I don't try to get up. There is no way I can win the race, stay in front of the hamster, so I give up and lie there quietly.

My breathing eases. My heartbeat slows. My mind clears. The hamster disappears. I am left with the slivered remnants of my life—me as a five-year-old sitting on the porch step waiting for my mother to come home, my drunk stepfather yelling at me at my tenth birthday party and his belt hitting my back, getting thrown out of high school for smoking in the girl's room, and the slap across my face from Paul, my first lover.

***

My precious boys—seven and nine—have held me together since their father deserted us six years ago. I've had boyfriends since, but none ever stayed around for long. I can't even have more kids; my mother insisted I get fixed years ago, bribed me with a hundred dollars. Dammit.

The police say I could have killed Ben and Cole and that I've abused and neglected them. I know better. My sister won't keep them for more than a week, so Ben and Cole are made temporary wards of the state and sent to foster care.

Some lady I don't know is taking care of my boys. The court order states I can only see them once a week, in a special building where social workers watch my every move and even take notes. I've lost all the privacy in my life. When I get out of this hellhole, I'll find my sons and steal them away.

Drugs and alcohol are my lifeblood. I started using pills, ones the doctor kept ordering for my back pain, after my auto accident ten years ago. I've come to depend on them to feel like a normal person and get rid of my terrible fears. I didn't know then what they would do to my life, how much they would mess it up and keep me from graduating from high school.

I am twenty-six. The exercise wheel in my mind goes too fast. I'm scared I can't do what the court wants me to do to get Ben and Cole back. I love my boys. The authorities tell me love is not enough; that I need to provide for them, protect them, discipline them, and get a job so I can support them. They tell me I'm not strong enough to take care of my beautiful sons, that since I was fired from the nursing home, I can't even take care of myself. So what that I stole some of those old ladies' jewelry; they don't know what they're wearing anyway. Like a goldfish in a bowl, my head swims in a sea of confusion.

Joe, I learn he's called a public defender, has scheduled another court appearance. I'm excited; maybe I can finally get Ben and Cole back and go home. A similar van takes me to court to stand before a judge. Joe tells the judge I have been a model prisoner and that this is only my second DUI offense, the first one with the children in the car, that I need to be given probation.

This time in court I pay more attention to what is going on and have a longer time to speak. I have to raise my right hand and swear to tell the truth, the whole truth, before I can talk. When I try to explain my situation, why I deserve my boys back, the judge interrupts and says, "Get a full-time job. Find your own place to live. Work on your education. You need at least a high school diploma. No matter how hard life is today, always choose the path that's best for you in the long term."

I want to tell him why I can't do those things, that it's hard for me to read and write, and how I need my boyfriend, Teddy, even if he hits me once in a while. That's only when he's drinking or I do something that's out of line. I tell him how scared I am to be by myself.

Eleanor, a grandma-type volunteer lady who visits the boys every three or four weeks to check on their welfare, talks next. "The boys deserve a safe and stable environment. Crystal hasn't proven she can provide that. They are adjusting well to their foster home."

I respond in a loud voice. "I don't understand what that lady is saying. I love my boys. I want them back. They belong to me. I'm their mother."

"Appeal denied." The judge isn't listening to me. He turns his head away and says, "Next."

I am left talking to myself. A court attendant in a uniform gently takes my arm and leads me back to my seat. I jerk my arm away. "Don't touch me," I say.

A social worker from the court directs me to a bench in the courthouse hallway and sits beside me. "I'll help you find an Alcoholics or Narcotics Anonymous. When you're out of rehab, you'll need the support. It's essential."

"I've been to those groups before. They don't work; they only make me want to use more."

"It's part of the treatment plan. You have to do it."

"Screw this," I mutter.

"No choices now, and you must complete the parenting course. It's only three hours a week. It meets at St. Paul's church, right off the city bus line. Here's your bus ticket allotment."

"Okay, I'll try." I take the six tickets and step away from her. I brush back my shoulder length hair, once soft and shiny but now coarse and stringy.

"Before you can even think about getting the boys back, you also need to take the anger management and domestic violence courses. Call this number or go online to sign up for them now, so you can start when you've completed the parenting class."

"I don't know how to use a computer and can't type, and my cell phone doesn't always work."

"I'll speak to your rehab director. Maybe she'll help you. At least, she can give you a pass to go to the library. You can use their computers for free."

I take a deep breath and jam my fists into my jean pockets. "I never used a computer. What do you do?"

"My God, you didn't learn computers in high school? I'll make sure you get approved for a class. The library teaches them several times a month."

I want to punch her, but I clench my fists and nod my head in agreement."

***

My mother visits me at the center. She hugs me, makes small talk, and then says, "You owe me money for the mobile home you and Teddy trashed. You need to get a job when you get out, something that pays at least ten dollars an hour, enough to pay me back." She forgets I don't even have a high school diploma. I don't remind her.

My sister, Angie, stops by. "I'm sorry I couldn't take care of the boys for you while you're in here. They were too disruptive when they stayed with us for those two days you were in jail. I told the social worker I couldn't handle them. Foster care will be better for them anyway."

"God damn you," I say. "You never even tried."

"I'm outta here." She grabs her purse off the table and stomps out of the room.

Teddy visits. The half-wit workers don't discover the stash hidden in his jacket pocket. He hands me the paper bag. "Come here, Baby. Give me some lovin' before I leave."

"No," I say. "You'll have to go now. I'm not in the mood." The bag only has three pills. I slip it under my bedspread.

"I drove all the way here to see you, make sure you got your stash. You goddamn well are going to make it worth my while."

I push him away and say, "Get out." God, how I hate him right now.

Just as the housemother comes down the hall, he leaves. I pull out a big calendar from the stack of papers on my table and start to fill in the squares for the different appointments.

There are not enough hours in the day for me to do what everyone wants. I scribble x's over most of the squares in my calendar. Then I walk over to my bed and lie down.

I close my eyes and see myself running on the exercise wheel. It's going faster and faster. The hamster is behind me. I feel his breath on my feet. I fall off. I try to get up but can't. I feel the little sucker's breath on my ankle. He bites my heel. I scream. My head jerks, and my eyes open wide. I am tangled in my sheets and blanket. My arms thrash. Ben and Cole's eyes pierce through my being. Soon the panic will come.

I reach for my Vicodin stash, street drugs Teddy brought that I hid inside a mattress tear. I grab all three pills and swallow them dry. Then I untangle my bed linens and reach under the bed for my special pillow. I relax. Ben and Cole's eyes fade. Soon the hamster also will go away. I will feel peace again.

***

Someone is shaking my shoulder. "Wake up, Crystal."

I try to open my eyes, but they flutter and then close. "Where am I?" I mumble.

"You're in bed in your room in Harvest House. A worker found you in your room lying on the floor beside your bed and called me. They suspected drugs and somehow got a sample of your urine. The results test came positive. They should throw you out of the program, but they like you and want to give you another chance."

The voice doesn't sound familiar, but it is warm and comforting.

"No drugs. I must have fallen," I mumble, glad that I'm alert enough to lie.

I open my eyes and see the picture of the man in red riding the black horse. A woman with short blonde hair and dressed in blue scrubs smiles down at me. "I'm Katie Adkins, the nurse here. The director just approved your participation in my research study."

Suddenly I feel more alert. "Research study?"

"An intensive program to help women struggling like you to get your life back on track. If you agree, I'll be the nurse working with you." She sits down and smiles at me. A kind look fills her eyes. "Tell me all that's happened," she says.

I find myself babbling, telling the nurse about the hamster wheel and losing Ben and Cole. She listens but doesn't offer advice or too much sympathy. I don't trust her but am happy when she agrees to see me again tomorrow.

***

After lunch the next day, she visits me in my room just as she promised. Even though I'm lying in bed, I feel better, I slept well last night and the hamster stayed away. Maybe it was the medicine she had a doctor order to help with my Vicodin addiction.

She sits on the sturdy wooden chair by my dresser and chats for a few minutes about the weather, and then asks, "How can I most help you?" That question surprises me. Others have never asked for my opinions. They tell me what to do without listening to my thoughts.

"First take that picture off the wall. Then, get me my boys back."

She walks over and takes the picture down. "That was easy but getting the boys back will require a lot of work. We'll figure how to start and take things one step at a time. The grant will allow us to meet for an hour three times a week for six months."

I shrug, not sure exactly what she means but trust her enough to say, "Okay." After all, she took the picture down without arguing.

***

But it isn't okay at first. To stay in her program, she insists I keep taking the medicine to stop my Vicodin cravings, complete the court required classes, attend a Narcotics Anonymous (NA) meeting, and stop seeing Teddy. "That's not fair," I complain. "They're my only pleasures. I refuse."

She tilts her head "I understood getting the boys back was more important than the drugs, but maybe not. Perhaps you're not right for the program." She picks up her briefcase from my bureau and starts out the door.

I sit for a minute thinking about what she said, and then run down the hallway to catch her. "I'm sorry. I know I have to change to get my boys. I'll try." Even though she is caring, she means business. I respect that.

First, Katie helps me use her office computer to set up the court required classes on parenting, domestic abuse, and anger management. She even gets me enough bus tickets to get back and forth to these classes and to the library to take a computer course. The day I finish the programs and receive my certificates, we have a little party in the center kitchen—root beer floats. We tell each other funny stories and laugh a lot.

Katie suggests I keep a journal of my day-to-day feelings, making sure to include past memories of Ben and Cole. Some days I write; some days I don't. Remembering the happy times makes me smile, especially the picnic we had last year to celebrate Ben's birthday. The times I neglected them or wasn't there for them make me cry. That I paid more attention to my boyfriends than my boys is unbelievable to me now. For Ben and Cole, I must heal and not do what my mother did to Angie and me.

She goes with me to several NA group meetings helping me find one I like. I choose a group with only women. Katie agrees I don't need to be tempted to get involved in another relationship with a man now. I need to build a relationship with myself first. I agree to allow Sara Perkins, a middle-aged single mom to be my sponsor.

Slowly, I work through NA's twelve step program, similar to the one of the Alcoholic Anonymous group. At first, I sit in the back of the room and don't participate. Listening to the other women's stories gives me hope and makes me feel like I'm not alone or a bad person but one that needs to change and can only do that with divine guidance. With everyone's encouragement, I slowly share my story. It takes two months for me to acknowledge God as a central figure in my life and that without His help; I am powerless over my addiction.

The group moderator asks, "Where do you feel the closest to God?"

Without hesitation, I say, "Outdoors, walking in the woods. For me, God and nature belong together."

I decide to spend a half-hour most days in a nearby park. Walking there gives me a sense of peace and helps me sort through my thoughts.

The NA group suggests phoning Mom and apologizing for how I'd hurt her. It takes some convincing from Sara, but I finally agree. Katie lets me use the phone in her office to make the call. My heart pounds. Praying the hamster won't come back, I clutch the phone, close my eyes, and take deep breaths like Katie has taught me, yet the hamster appears in the corner of my mind. I keep breathing slowly and steadily. He starts to run on the wheel but falls off on the third spoke. My heartbeat slows. The hamster disappears.

I open my eyes and press on the numbers. Mom picks up on the second ring. "Can you stop by for a visit? I need to talk to you." I hear reluctance in her voice. Maybe she thinks I'm going to ask her for money, my usual reason for such a call.

"I'm off work early tomorrow afternoon. I'll come about four," she says.

Katie receives permission for me to use the facility's kitchen for the visit and suggests I serve cookies and coffee to make Mom feel welcome. The next morning I walk to Walmart to buy pecan sandies, Mom's favorite, then spent the afternoon fixing my hair and dressing in my best clothes, black slacks, and a beige turtleneck. Katie's promise to be available in the next room should I need her helps me relax.

"Crystal," she says, "Working through your resentments with your mother will help you learn about yourself and better parent the boys. Second chances. We all need them at one time or another. Even your mother deserved that. Sometimes, parents do the best they can even though it's not enough."

I remember the NA's focus on forgiveness and agree to try to better understand Mom.

I watch for her out the center's front window and meet her on the doorstep. She arrives five minutes early. We hug briefly, and I escort her into the kitchen. She stares at me for several seconds before we sit down at the table. "You look wonderful, Crystal, the best I've seen you in years."

Is she being sarcastic? I'm not sure, but I smile and say, "Thank you." All the while I pray the hamster will stay away.

She wipes her glasses and sets them on the table. "The program here must be helping." She takes a cookie off the plate.

"I'm trying. It's been hard." A shadowy image of the hamster crosses my mind. I resist calling for Katie and take several deep breaths. The hamster disappears.

"I don't have extra money if that's what this is about." She frowns.

"It's not about money. It's about *us*. I want us to get along. We've had problems. I know I wasn't the easiest child to raise, but it could have been worse." I stir sugar into my coffee.

She takes a tissue from her purse. "That's true."

I force myself to forge ahead. "I want to apologize for the trailer Teddy and I trashed. I'm not seeing him anymore."

"You and Teddy broke up. Good. He was a bad influence."

"What we did was wrong. I'm sorry."

She dabs her eyes with the tissue. "I'm partly to blame. I tried to make up for the guilt of not being there for you when you were a kid. Part of me knew you and Teddy couldn't manage the trailer, but I bought it for you anyway, hoping for the best."

"Nonetheless, we blew a golden opportunity to straighten ourselves out."

Tears are running down both our cheeks. "You know, Crystal, this feels like the first honest conversation we've had in years. I've always loved you but am sorry I was more interested in my boyfriends than you girls. I changed several years ago. I'm no longer chasing men. I never told you, but I joined a women's support group. The nurse running it helped me see the light." She reaches across the table for my hand.

"Let's start over again," I say. The hamster has completely disappeared.

She nods. "My car is outside. Why don't we go to Panera's for an early dinner and talk more. I have a lot of explaining to do."

I smile. "All right, but first I need to get the housemother's permission."

***

The following week I use Harvest House's computer to e-mail Angie. "Part of my treatment program is making amends for what I've done wrong. Need to talk to you. Can we meet in the park Sunday afternoon?"

She e-mails back. "Busy that day. Sorry."

I want to give up but Katie encourages me to persist, and so I do. All the bickering Angie and I have done throughout the years has to end.

Eventually, partly because Mom has encouraged Angie to reconnect, we meet at the park close to Harvest House. The night before our date, the hamster comes back. I wake up screaming in the middle of the night. Katie has taught me what to do—visualizing him too weak and powerless to even get on the hamster wheel. I lie quietly, breathe slowly and deeply and see the hamster lying on the ground. Soon he creeps away.

Angie waits on the park bench when I arrive. We talk, sometimes yelling, sometimes whispering, and sometimes crying. I can't remember who said what. *Mom loved you more than me. You always hated me. You stole my boyfriend. You started the rumor I was a slut. Sometimes I wished you were dead.*

An hour later, I wave my hands in front of her face and say, "Stop. Let make a deal to get along and talk to each other in a normal way, get to know each other again. I'm sorry I told you to 'piss off' on your last visit. That was wrong."

"I felt bad about that. I need you, Crystal, the way you used to be."

"I'm trying hard. I've been clean for four months. Only two months left in the program. My nurse, Katie, has helped me change my life, find out who I really am."

Angie bites her lip. "I've felt guilty about walking out and refusing to take the boys. I'd like to do that now. Have them leave the foster mother and come live with Tony and me. After all, we're family. Family helps family."

"You'd do that?" I say. "Really take them to live with you day in and day out?"

"Uh-huh. I'll look into it. Once our home is approved by the state, they can come."

I'm so overwhelmed, I can hardly breathe. "Then, I can see them more."

"Probably so," she says as she looks at her watch. "I'd better get going. Gotta pick up my kids from school."

I walk to the corner and wait for the light to change. I smile. Angie's changed. She cares. I hum Dave Matthew's song, "Sister," all the way home.

***

I don't hear from Angie for a week. I e-mail her twice and then phone her.

"I hate to tell you this, Crystal, but Tony won't agree to take the boys." Her voice shakes. "And I don't want them either. I spoke without thinking the other day. We can't afford our girls to be exposed to you know, all the problems. Probably better you and I don't see each other anymore. It's too hard. I get a migraine when I'm with you."

I can almost see the smug look on her face. "But you promised and I trusted you." My stomach hardens. "You're the bitch you always were. Setting me up and letting me down. You and your family shit. You're no sister. You're a screw-up. Go to hell. I hope your migraines last the rest of your life." My heart pounds as I slam the phone down.

***

The hamster panic gets bad. I wake up at night with his teeth biting my heel. In the daytime, he relentlessly chases me. I need my Vicodin. I sneak out of the Harvest House after curfew to hunt for a pay phone. I need to call Teddy to bring me more drugs. I walk around for a while until I remember an old pay phone near a dilapidated gas station. I call Teddy. A computer voice answers, "The number you have dialed has been disconnected." Son of a bitch. I slam down the phone, sit down in the booth, and sob.

133

Someone is knocking on the glass. What if it's a cop? I panic and check my pockets for drugs. Oh, I'm still clean. Thank God, he can't arrest me. I look up. It's not a cop. It's another street person who wants to use the phone, a woman strung out like I used to be.

Her presence shocks me. What was I thinking trying to call Teddy? Thank God he didn't answer. I open the door.

"You all right, sister?" the woman asks. She is unsteady on her feet and leans against the glass.

I nod and breathe in the fresh air. In my mind, I force the hamster to run out of the phone booth and reach in my pocket, where Sara Perkins' phone number is. "I'll be out in a minute," I tell the woman.

Sara answers on the second ring.

"I need you right now," I mumble, then tell her the cross streets where the gas station's located.

"Wait right where you are. I'll be there in a jiffy."

Ten minutes later she pulls up in her Ford Focus. "Hop in," she says. "I'm taking you back to the center."

The hamster is biting my heels. "No, no, they'll throw me out of the program for breaking curfew."

"I phoned them before leaving home. They understand. They're on your side. Since you haven't used, it will be all right."

Her voice calms me. I tell her about my sister and what a jerk she is. She listens and says, "You know, Crystal, the same thing happened to me many years ago. You have to forge on without your sister's support."

"But I was so happy Angie would have the boys, that they'd be with family."

"Best she doesn't take them if she doesn't want them," Sara says.

I sigh and wipe the tears from my face. "Yeah."

Back at the center, the housemother is waiting for us at the door. "I'm disappointed you left like that and that you didn't tell us how upset you were. Sara phoned. She's taking responsibility." She hands me a paper cup. "If your urine test is clean, we'll forget about this night," she says.

My urine test comes back clean. I walk back up to my room, lie down in bed and fall asleep. The hamster doesn't bother me the entire night.

Katie talks to me the next day and listens to my falling-out with Angie and my experience in the phone booth. She explains that's it common for family members to be estranged when there are problems like mine. "It's up to you to move forward. Keep your mind focused on your goal, getting Ben and Cole back.

Tears well up in my eyes. "It's just so hard."

"What else can we do to help? she asks.

"Something else to stop this anxiety and panic when the hamster comes. I don't know what else to do." My voice shakes.

She runs her fingers through her hair. "How 'bout a yoga class? Yoga can be very relaxing."

I nod and agree, just to please her.

It is hard to go at first. But now that I'm three weeks into the class, I realize Katie is right. Yoga is very relaxing and has helped keep the hamster away.

***

Katie encourages me to go back to court to obtain visitation rights for the boys. "What if I panic in there? What if the hamster comes back?" I ask.

"I'll be standing right beside you, telling the judge about the progress you've made. Look at all you've accomplished. You've stayed clean. You've been faithful in taking your medication to control your addiction. And you finished all your required classes."

I smile. "Don't forget to mention I've been studying for my GED."

"I will and also that you have already scheduled a date next month to take the test."

"I think of the boys every day. They let me talk on the phone to the boys at the foster mom's house. Ben sounds okay. Cole whimpers a lot. They say they love me and can't wait 'til I get well. I believe them."

***

I meet with my public defender, Joe, who agrees to present my request to the judge. The day my petition is to be heard, Katie and I arrive at the courthouse early.

My legs tremble as I stand in front of the judge's podium in the courtroom, but I speak with assurance and passion. He grants me a half-day's visitation every week with the boys. The only stipulation he makes is that Katie must supervise.

I feel strong and competent as I walk out of the courtroom. The hamster never shows his face.

***

For that first visit with the boys, Katie and I walk to the park to meet them. The foster mom drives up and opens the car door to let Ben and Cole out. My mouth drops open. They've grown so much. They run toward me. I reach out my arms and engulf them in a huge bear hug.

I sit between them on the swing set. The three of us are pumping to see which one of us can go the highest. Ben wins. We all laugh. An ice cream truck passes by. I look at Katie. She reaches in her pocket, pulls out a five-dollar bill and hands it to me. I buy us all an ice cream sandwich. We sit on the grass and snuggle while we eat. The boys tell me about their new school and the new friends they've met. I'm sad not to be part of their life now but smile, knowing that soon, if I stay clean, I'll get them back.

When Katie points to her watch and motions to me, I tell the boys, "It's time for us to say good-bye. I've been very sick but am getting better every day. Once I'm all well, we'll go back home and live together again. It won't be long now."

Both Ben and Cole cry. I put an arm around each one as I walk them to the car.

After the foster mom drives away, Katie and I sit on the park bench for a few minutes. "Never again will I do anything to lose my boys. Thank God the hamster is finally dead. With Sara and your help, I've killed it," I say.

She pauses. "Yes, we've been there for you, but you're the one who made this all happen. It's your story, Crystal. Your victory."

***

Katie hugs me hard the day she leaves to go back to her regular health department job. Remembering my panic attacks and the hamster chasing me makes my voice choke. "I'll never forget you," I say.

She shakes her head. "No, it's the other way around. You've been my inspiration. I never told you but years ago, I also had an addiction problem. I injured my neck in an auto accident, and a doctor prescribed opioids for the pain. I let it get out of control. If it wasn't for the help of my nursing supervisor, I'd have lost my nurse's license. Working with you made me stronger and better able to understand and forgive myself. So, thank you, Crystal, for all that you are."

"My God, Katie. Here I thought I was the taker, but it's been a two-way street."

"That's life, Crystal. We're here to help each other."

Dear Reader,

I hope you enjoyed these short stories. If you have a minute, it would mean a lot to me if you wrote a review on Amazon. Thank you. I really appreciate your support.

Lois Gerber